It Started Like This

Tales of First Words, First Dates,
and Love at First Sight

Six Novelettes
by
Raven Easton

CONTENTS

The Poodle and the Pug

1

PATRICE BARRETT HEARD a man's voice.

"Your dog is beautiful," it said.

She looked up from her seat on the park bench to see a man walking a pug. "Oh, thank you," she said.

"You don't see a lot of standard poodles these days," the man said, "but I've always liked them. Especially when they have a regular poodle cut and not all the frou-frou you see at the shows." The man's voice was rough, but he spoke clearly.

"They call it a puppy cut," she said, "even though it doesn't have much to do with puppies."

"Clean face, clean paws, but you gotta have the curly head and the pom on the tail," the man said. "Gotta have some poodly features on a poodle. Yours is a picture. Standards look great in black. Hey, Warren," he said, "look how that dog sits there all dignified."

Patrice said, "Your dog's name is Warren?"

"Yeah," the man said.

"Your dog is very cute," she said. Although Patrice di

not think pugs were cute, and she did not think this one was cute.

What she did think was that this man was Exhibit 1 in support of the proposition that people look like their dogs. He was short but very broad. He gave the impression of wideness from the top of his head to his ankles, if that were even possible. Most of him was muscle – you could tell it through his neck. It was not a fat guy's neck; his head was attached to his shoulders like the Sphinx to its slab. Like his nervous little pug, there was some male energy close to the surface that gave him an air of alertness.

While his face was a little puggy, too – it was flat and it made his eyes look large and wide-spaced – there was a softness to those eyes, and they were blue. His black hair was thick and curly and cut short, a good pro job on what had to be a challenge for the stylist, with some wires of grey throughout. Impressive eyebrows. He was jowly but those jowls were clean-shaven, probably only a few hours before. Clearly, Patrice observed, this man attended to his appearance with some care.

But she still didn't much care for pugs, and while she had not been interested in dog talk or any talk with this man, after looking him over with her customary cool-eyedness, she had to admit: He fit a lot of appeal into a pretty efficient package, even if that package was on the squarish side.

"Hey!" the man spoke sharply to the pug. "Leave Beatrice alone!"

Warren had taken the opportunity of a slackened leash to make a beeline for the poodle's hindquarters for an investigatory sniff. The poodle stood and twirled to check out

Warren's scent, but found the pug's backside too low down and scooting out of range as he stayed with the poodle's now moving target, with the result that the dogs were circling each other, their leashes tangling.

The man said, "I am so, so sorry." He scooped Warren up and freed his leash from the poodle's.

"That's all right," Patrice said, although it wasn't. "At least their tails were wagging and there was no nipping."

"It's a natural thing," the man said, "but it's no way to say hello to a prize like Beatrice or, for that matter, her mistress."

"How did you know her name is Beatrice?" Patrice said.

"It's embroidered on her collar," he said. "Took a chance that was her name."

Patrice felt a little foolish. "Ah, so it is," she said. "Yes, Beatrice."

"I try to make him behave in civilized company," the man said. "I thought that when you get a male dog fixed he doesn't have such an interest in a bitch's scent." The man recoiled. "I'm sorry for using that word. I intended to use it in a technical sense."

"Don't worry about it," Patrice said. "Dogs get a lot more than sexual information from the butt-sniffing, so neutering wouldn't affect that. And, of course, Beatrice has been spayed herself so she's not – I'm trying to think of a nice phrase for it – smelling sexy."

And, Patrice thought, Beatrice could sometimes be a bitch in a non-technical sense. And she had forgotten, and did not care to attempt to recall, what non-sexual information canine butt-sniffing might convey.

"Yeah," the man said, somewhat sadly. "Neutering has

never seemed to have had any positive effect on his behavior at all. He still falls in love with nearly every pant leg he sees," he said, holding the excited Warren even more closely as he noticed that Patrice was wearing some stylish jeans.

Patrice was beginning to wish that the man and his wiggly dog would move on. He seemed a bit . . . common, but a nice common. He hadn't said or done anything objectionable, he was dressed in very nice – even stylish – casual clothes that fit his fireplug body surprisingly well, and he seemed sincerely regretful that Warren had not given a better account of himself.

But Patrice had been enjoying the late fall afternoon in Central Park with Beatrice, trying to add to her collection of New York City wildlife photographs – mostly birds, but she'd snagged a coyote, a possum, and a feral tabby – and was about ready to wrap the day with a few minutes of watching the human fauna go by from her vantage on the park bench. She preferred to be alone with her thoughts, although she couldn't remember what she was thinking when the man appeared and spoke admiringly of Beatrice.

Maybe trying to be friendly with the guy was a mistake. She couldn't tell if he was trying to flirt with her.

It surprised her to feel a slight annoyance when she realized that it didn't seem like he was.

But he was still standing there.

2

Now there, Leo DeGiulia thought, is a woman.

That is what a woman should look like.

At least, that is what a woman draped serenely over a

park bench on a path trailing along the mid-Eighties in Central Park should look like.

That this one happened to be rolling up on the fringes of middle age meant nothing.

More than classy.

Classic.

Slim. Dressed right, with the black jeans and turtleneck. Tan denim jacket. Hair not too short, not too long, and not colored in a shade that her skin tattled on. Tall, taller than he was, quite a bit taller, with those angles in the face that photographers love. A scarf to match the jacket with the ends trailing off to one side for that put-together look and one that postpones a view of the neck for some other time.

Her posture was both formal and relaxed, like a royal who knows she might be photographed at any time, but lives her life and deals with it.

And that was a nice camera with a nice lens, and she had a strong strap for it and looped it across her chest like she knew what she was doing.

And she had a classy dog.

And she was talking to him.

He asked, "Is that the D850 or the 810?"

"Oh," she said after a moment, "the camera. It's an 810."

"Nice," he said. "I have a 750, but I wished I'd have gotten your camera or waited for the 850. Although with my skills, the extra pixels are wasted on me."

"The 750s are great cameras, too. What do you photograph?"

"Mostly Warren," he said. "See what I mean?"

"Oh, come on."

Leo said, "It's like a lot of things. I'm retired, looking for things to do, what do men do? They buy toys. I go out and get a nice camera and a decent lens. Study up on how to use it, which basically means I leave it in auto mode the whole time, aim it, and press the button. I go out one fine morning and take pictures of buildings and Warren, go home, look at them, and forget about it. Same with the bicycle, riding downtown is scary and I'm not exactly mister balance on two wheels, so it sits in my foyer. Looks good there. Same with the telescope. You can't see stars from SoHo and I look out on what, maybe a couple of buildings? Stupid. But it's a fancy telescope and it looks nice sitting next to the window."

Patrice thought: *I don't really ever look at the pictures I take, either.* "You live downtown?" she said.

"Yeah," he said. "Warren and I drive up here a couple of times a week if I'm feeling lucky about parking. Even if I'm not, to be honest. Another dumb thing, having a car in the city. But I bought a unit with parking, you know, for the resale, and a car comes in handy if I want to get out of town. And, like I said, Warren and I come up here. You can only take a dog on the subway if it's in a carrier. Forget about it. I'd rather try to bathe a mongoose, and he'd howl and yap the whole way up here. Cabs and Ubers, hit and miss if the driver allows pets. So, with Miss Beatrice there, you must live fairly close?"

Leo immediately regretted the question. He wanted to know more about this woman sitting languidly on the bench, but he didn't want to seem too forward. He was aware that his appearance and the sound of his voice was sometimes frightening to women. He had practiced speaking well and in recent years had read widely to improve his knowledge of all the worlds and peoples that come together in New York City. He got a little dog instead of a big dog.

Would she answer? She did not respond right away, had looked away and seemed to be thinking.

She said, "Yes. The Majestic down on 72nd and the Park."

"Beautiful," he said. "Incredible place. When I moved to Manhattan I looked at Central Park West but at the time I never would have qualified at The Majestic. What a history."

Leo was embarrassed that he had not checked for a wedding ring. Places at The Majestic started at mid-seven figs. A single woman could certainly live there, but . . . .

No ring.

"Yes," she said, "you're always going to get some interesting people living in these great old buildings along the Park. I used to run into Conan O'Brien in the lobby, he was always really nice. I'm probably dating myself, but Milton Berle grabbed my ass more than once when Lorna wasn't around."

"I heard that about Berle," Leo said. "Sorry. I hope times have changed."

"My ass certainly has," she said.

Leo was so surprised at this sudden self-deprecation from this long cool woman that he laughed, which would have been a natural reaction to her joke except that he was aware that his laugh was harsh like his voice, and could be a little frightening, too, and he tried to suppress it around women.

He said, "I suppose a gentleman would deny that, but, of course, it would imply an inappropriate familiarity with your, you know," he said. "I have better manners than Warren."

It was her turn to laugh.

"I always wanted to stop by the lobby there at The Majestic," he said, "soak up a little history. You probably know that's where Chin Gigante tried to kill Frank Costello, but the bullet just grazed his skull. Didn't kill him but it was a huge event in the New York mob. Costello took the hint and retired as head of the Luciano family – Charley Lucky, they called Luciano. He was in prison at the time, not so lucky. Vito Genovese took over, which was the whole idea behind the shooting. Gigante eventually headed that family, despite his lousy aim."

"I didn't know that," she said. "Wasn't he the guy who walked around in his pajamas acting crazy?"

"Yes, he was," Leo said. "Good memory. Luciano and Meyer Lansky and I think also Lepke Buchalter lived in your building at one time or another."

"You know a lot about the Mafia," she said.

"My last name is DeGiulia," he said. "I'm Leo DeGiulia. Yeah, actually a lot of Italians have blue eyes. Even though my people are from the south originally, around Taranto. That's actually in the Puglia part of Italy, although that's not why I got a pug. My father wasn't in organized crime, and I'm not – never was – and he always told us that none of the family was connected. But a couple of the uncles and great-uncles were a little mysterious, me and my brothers and sisters were never quite sure. Actually, I was pretty sure. I got interested and read up on some history and saw there were a couple-three DeGiulias associated way low-down the totem pole with the Bonnano family and in Philly. Not made, not even connected, just 'associated,' as the cops say. In other words, they would run an errand now and then for connected guys, and in return they were allowed to run a scam here and there, a craps game or something. Small potatoes stuff. It's not a common Italian name, so when you see it somewhere in connection with the mob, you wonder. But no, nothing to do with me."

"I'll be honest," she said, "I wondered a little about you by the way you said 'forget about it.'"

"Eh, fuhgeddabahdit," he said, allowing a little growl into his voice.

Patrice scooted a little to the right on the bench and gave Beatrice a soft shove with her foot to make room.

"Why don't you sit for a bit, Leo?" she said. "I'm Patrice Barrett."

3

PATRICE THOUGHT LEO seemed a little taken aback by the invitation. He thanked her and said he would be right back after making sure Warren had done one of the things he came to do. He tossed a green plastic bag in the trash on his way back and had Warren under one arm.

So now they were flirting, a little. It still felt friendly and not a prelude to any kind of invitation, but it was still flirting. It felt good. She hadn't done it in a while, but this guy had turned out to be cool and funny, in an offbeat way. Kind of shy, but he was hanging in there. A little rough, good-cop rough, not dock-boss rough. And they were outdoors in public and near her home so she was in a position to put an end to it if it went the wrong way or she got bored. The sun had drifted behind the buildings and was heading into the Hudson; it would be dark soon and she wouldn't be sitting there for long, so no need to let the guy just stand there.

Leo reminded her a little of her late husband. A little mysterious, a little unfinished. Smarter than he looked. Better-off than he acted. Leo even looked a little like him, even built a little like him, although Leo was a little more of everything, including a little shorter. She had given some thought to divorcing that husband on grounds of boredom and serial grumpiness and some other serial things she suspected him of and was considering hiring a private investigator to look into, but she was still only considering it when he stroked out after a squash game at the Yale Club. Karma, maybe, since he'd become a member without even knowing what state Yale was in. Adroit estate planning left her with more money and revenue than any divorce settlement could have.

Since then, she'd had dates with men she met through friends or through her charity boards, and a couple were associates of her late husband. She had liked a few of them, but after two or three dates they would stop calling, and the next she heard they had been seen around town squiring someone younger and blonder and more comfortable with surgery.

"Okay, Warren," Leo said, "we've been invited to sit with these ladies but if you bother Beatrice you'll have to sniff mutt butts down at Columbus Park for the next month." Warren snuffled and coughed at being spoken to in that fashion, but when Leo set him down he walked over to Beatrice, who was still sitting, and looked up at her. She looked down at him and wagged her tail once. Then she wagged it one more time. Then she opened her mouth and panted three times, betraying a slight poodle smile before closing up again. Warren laid down in front of her and was quiet.

"Beatrice is as regal as her name," Leo said.

Patrice said, "You said you were retired? What did you —"

"That dog is a faggot."

Leo and Patrice looked up to see three skinny late-teen boys, each carrying a skateboard, walking past and laughing.

"Hey!" Leo said. "Hey, the three of youse!"

The three kept walking, but the laughing stopped.

"It's okay," Patrice said. "Just punks."

"Punks for sure," Leo said, "but there's no such thing as 'just punks.' I've known a lotta punks."

"Really, don't," she said, and reached out and touched his sleeve.

"Warren," he stage-hissed, "stay! You too, Beatrice."

With that, and with the dogs frozen by his tone, Leo rocketed off the bench and at a speed Patrice could barely believe covered the ground to the punks and passed them, whirling to face them as he did. The punks stopped.

Leo glared at the tall punk in the middle, all arms and legs and skateboarder's muscle. He was the one who had spoken. "You got a problem with the hearing?" Leo said, tapping his ear. He spoke in a growling whisper, but loud enough for Patrice to hear.

The middle punk was a head-and-a-half taller than Leo. The two other punks were softer but heavier, and also taller than Leo. They tossed their heads every few seconds to move the greasy hair from their eyes. "Hey, man, what the fuck?" the tall middle punk said.

Leo looked each one in the eye in quick turn. "First one of youse to show a weapon, or who tries to pass me," he whispered, "I'm gonna put all three of youse down. You know what that means on the West Side, to put somebody down?" Leo shifted his position very slightly, but so abruptly and with such speed, that each of the punks startled.

The punks said nothing. Leo said, "You better hope you don't find out."

"Hey, just get the fuck out of our way, man," the tall middle punk said.

Leo said, "First rule – hey, you listening? Look at me – first rule is, no swearing. No fucks, no shits, no damns or goddams, no motherfuckers, and no cocksuckers. And no bitches. That's a lady sitting there. Second rule is, you will refer to me as 'sir,' not 'man' or anything other than 'sir.' You all clear on that? Just nod your heads."

Left punk and right punk nodded slightly. Tall middle punk continued to look down at Leo.

"What's your name?" Leo said.

The tall middle punk dropped his skateboard to the ground but before he could mount it to spin and escape, Leo shot his foot out and stepped on one end of it, the other end rising easily into his hand.

"Hey!" the punk said. "You can't steal my board, you old fuck! I'm gonna call the cops."

"I'll let that one go," Leo said, "since I surprised you and you may not have had time to remember to call me 'sir' and not to say fuck, you little prick."

"Hey, you swore!"

"My rule is, and I'm the only one here making rules, is that none of *youse* is allowed to swear."

"You can't just take my board," the punk said.

"And yet," Leo said, and he waved the board in his enormous hand.

The tall middle punk snaked out his hand toward the board, but Leo was faster. He smacked the punk's hand away, hard, making sure to bang his large right-hand ring on the punk's knuckle, then waggled his finger at him. "Try that one more time," he said. He looked at left and right punk as he waggled to remind them that he hadn't forgotten them and that his orders applied to them as well.

"Give it back!"

"I was concerned you were thinking about leaving before we had finished our business here," Leo said. He was still using the same menacing rasp.

"I'm gonna call the cops."

"You reach for any part of your clothing, and that goes for the two of youse, too," he whispered, nodding to the two flanking punks, "I'm going to assume you're going for a weapon, then you're all three down hard and long. Got that?"

The punks said nothing.

"Besides," Leo said, "we haven't found out your name yet. Tell you what: Here's mine." Leo pulled out his wallet and held up his driver's license. "Leo DeGiulia. Ring a bell?"

This time all three shook their heads.

"I don't think youse are going to call the cops," Leo said. "Let's take a look at this skateboard. Baker, good brand, okay board. I go for the Powell-Peralta, myself. No, I don't think you're gonna call the cops." Leo spun the board to display its bottom. "I noticed when you were holding it that someone named Lil Jahleel has burnt his name into the bottom of this board here. See that? Now unless your name is Lil Jahleel, which you can prove to me by showing me some ID, you ripped off this board from some poor kid."

"My name is none of your fu – none of your business," middle punk said.

"I know the neighborhood where Lil Jahleel probably lives," Leo said. "You know who also lives in neighborhoods like Lil Jahleel's?"

The left punk spoke for the first time. "No, sir."

"Big Jahleels." Leo turned to the left punk. "That's the way to do it, sir," he said. "You show respect, you get respect. Your colleague here . . . ."

"He's always talkin'," right punk said.

"I think those neighborhoods would be interested to know where I got Lil Jahleel's board," Leo whispered.

Tall middle punk snorted. "They don't know us."

A bright flash exploded behind the punks in the gathering dusk and they all turned their heads to it. Patrice pushed the button again, and a second flash caught them all.

"Got 'em," Patrice said. She held up the camera to show them the image that was lingering on the LCD screen. She was too far away for them to see much other than three illuminated ovals at the top of the screen.

"Excellent," Leo said. "Now, Stretch," he said, addressing the tall middle punk, and putting a little volume behind his whisper, "you may not be aware of this if you haven't read a newspaper in the last twenty years, but we do not call anyone or anything a faggot anymore. It's offensive and hurtful. Now you're aware of it. So before I let you gentlemen go, you, Stretch, being the talker, are going to apologize to this lady and her dog."

"Huh," Stretch said. "I heard her say it was okay. She didn't care."

"I care," Leo whispered. "And see that little dog there? That's my dog. My dog likes her dog very much. Are you calling my dog a faggot?"

"Come on, man" Stretch said, "I ain't apologizin' for shit."

Leo dropped the skateboard and jumped in the air – Patrice was astonished at the height he achieved – and landed with his entire mass on the center of the board, shattering it. Leo picked up the board and twisted it into two pieces. He held up the two pieces, jagged edges up.

"You are, Stretch, and you're going to do it now."

"That's my board!"

"No," Leo said. "You stole it. You just admitted it. It was never yours. I took it from you; actually, I just picked it up when you put it on the ground. I have as much right to it as you did, but since I have possession, it is more mine than yours. And I wanted to bust it. Now that we've set you straight on the legalities, Stretch, we're going to walk over to that bench and you're going to apologize." Right punk snickered. Right and left punk had scooted about a sneaker-length back and away from middle punk. "And it had better be sincere to my satisfaction." Leo waved the splintered edges of Lil Jahleel's board menacingly. "And then you can all go."

Left punk said, "Can I apologize for all of us? Sir?" he added.

"That's a nice show of friendship to Stretch here," Leo

said, "and nice respect to me, which I appreciate, but no. Stretch has the mouth. How about it, Stretch? End this? Don't forget the sincerity."

Stretch glowered at Leo. His alternatives were not attractive. He shuffled over to the bench.

"I apologize," he said to Patrice.

"For?" Leo whispered.

"I apologize for calling your dog a faggot."

"I accept your apology," Patrice said.

Stretch started to turn away.

"You're not done," Leo said. "The dog." Stretch threw his hands in the air and took a breath to object. But Leo growled, "Don't say another word to me, Stretch, not another word. You got nowhere you need to be and nowhere I'm going to let you go anyway. Just finish what you came over here to do. Sincere, now."

Left punk and right punk both snickered.

Stretch stayed where he was but turned his head to the black poodle. He said, "I'm sorry I called you a faggot."

"Beatrice?" Leo said.

The poodle yawned and licked her chops, panted a few times.

"You're lucky," Leo said. "Beatrice took apart the last punk who disrespected her. She's done with you."

"I suppose you want me to apologize to your dog for implying he's a faggot," Stretch sneered.

"Nah," Leo said. "Tell you the truth, I'm not so sure about him." Warren had been eyeing Stretch's bare leg. He now looked up in alarm and made a phlegmy sound.

"Let's go," Stretch said to left and right punk.

"I'm keeping the board," Leo whispered, "in case youse

think you might want to bring a po-lice back here. And I may want to visit a Big Jahleel or two of my acquaintance with that board and that photograph if you aren't out of my sight in thirty seconds. And gentlemen?"

The three stopped and looked at Leo.

"You thinking of maybe rolling through this area again offering observations about respectable park visitors as you dream about maybe getting a learner's permit someday?" he whispered. "Fuhgeddabahdit."

4

LEO AND PATRICE watched the punks walk away. Left and right punk were laughing and punched Stretch in his skateboard-free arms.

Leo looked at Patrice.

"I don't know whether to laugh or be frightened," she said. "I'm smiling and I don't seem to be scared. Come, sit."

"Sorry," Leo said.

"I sensed you were putting – well, I've got to ask," she said. "Did I hear you say 'youse'?"

Leo chuckled quietly. "Yeah."

"What does putting somebody down mean on the West Side?"

"No idea."

"Any reason those kids should have heard your name?"

"No."

"And the voice?"

"So they would listen carefully."

"And so you'd sound like The Godfather."

Leo smiled. "Maybe."

"What about the thing with the skateboard? Nice move to snag it."

"I'd laid down the law on language and the punk was calling my bluff. I could have slapped him but I wasn't going to touch him, there was never going to be any physical violence unless he started it. He had basically admitted to stealing the skateboard, so I improvised. I was scared I wouldn't be able to break it. But I ended up with a couple of weapons and made him think I was willing to blow my stack. That sealed the deal on him apologizing."

"Do you really have that skateboard you mentioned?"

"I told you about my toys," he said. "I boarded around downtown a little a half-dozen years ago or so, around the Battery sometimes. Probably looked pretty funny. Warren, don't say a word."

"These two are being unusually good," Patrice said. "I guess I should only speak for Beatrice."

"No," Leo said, "you're right, Warren too. Maybe he knows he's uptown. Behaving. Except for that butt-sniffing."

Patrice's curiosity had ramped up as she watched Leo flummox the punks. "I was going to ask you what you had been doing before you retired," she said. "You're certainly in shape enough to outflank those young men. Nothing wrong with your reflexes, either." *Or your brains.*

"Oh, that," he said. "I wrestled at Columbia."

"Columbia," she said. "No wonder you speak well."

"Nah," he said. "I was a scholarship kid from Newark when Newark was actually a place. Not a scholar. Not really much of a student."

"Well," she said, "you had to have had some kind of career."

"I always thought of it as a job," he said. "'Career' sounds so white collar or artsy. After I graduated I didn't really have anything I wanted to do. I went to work for a major nationwide security company. Private investigations. Because I looked strong and was strong and knew how to handle myself I was given some bodyguard assignments and I ended up guarding some pretty valuable bodies. Rockers, big acts from further back, actors, models, the occasional politician or rich guy or woman. Worked security at some clubs and events, too. You look at enough celebrity photos on the internet, you'll see me or a piece of me. But I stuck with it, the company was stable, I got a lot of repeat requests for my services. And some very nice tips under the table to make sure I was available next time the act came to town. With that and the pension and other savings, I decided I'd retire. Sometimes I think maybe it was a mistake. Too soon. Had some fun, some close calls too. Flushed a lot of drugs and evicted a lot of hookers and kept a lot of secrets."

"You could write a book," Patrice said.

"Could," he said. "Won't. A lot of those acts became friends. And personally, I felt like the job came with a certain understanding about confidentiality, like part of what they're paying for is their ability to trust my discretion. So I never said a word about any of them to anyone who asked, and I've had hundreds of requests for interviews. They knew the way I felt and they appreciated it. I still hear from some of those people when they roll through town. I'll do a private gig now and then for some of them, some big stars and the occasional newcomer, actually some decent paychecks in retirement, but the years . . . ."

"What did you mean about knowing a lot of punks?"

He laughed and looked away, as though thinking back. "Punk music itself, I mean real punk punk, CBGB, Mudd Club, Max's, was pretty gone before I started working security at clubs and concerts. My beat was heavy metal, death metal, grunge, thrash, emo. And the big arena and club acts from last century still working. Big pop acts. Most of the characters on stage were actually pretty cool customers. Almost all were accomplished musicians, some real pros, basically acting the part of badass rocker. Even the women. A surprising number didn't drink or take drugs. Some of the fans, though. Whoo. Thought rock-and-roll was an actual lifestyle. Some of those lads needed a hug from old Leo from time to time to remind them of their fondness for oxygen. And you'd still see a lot of punks, to answer your question. And by that I don't necessarily mean 1970s-type punks with the spiky hair and body piercings, although you do still see some of those – it's almost nostalgic now. I just mean aimless young men – not so many women – who had nothing to do but board during the day like those boys and go to clubs and shows at night. Some had money, some didn't. Never had huge trouble with them. Anything looked like trouble, they were easy to distract and redirect. And they were drug-skinny and didn't carry weapons and were not going to mess with me."

He was quiet for a moment. "That's a few years ago now. No rough stuff in my life for a while. But those three . . . . I'm sorry if I frightened you."

"It's okay," Patrice said. "Maybe you made a difference today, even though Stretch would never let you see it."

"Maybe."

"Was the sex scene around the bands as wild as we all

thought?" Patrice had grown curious about his relationships. If any.

"With the new bands, the younger rock acts, yes. With the older bands and the reunion tours, and the big pop acts, not so much. The more established bands have strong professional management that keeps a pretty tight lid on backstage partying. The newer acts trying to break through, though, they're mostly broke. When you've got nothing you're not so worried about paternity suits and VD. They got into rock-and-roll in the first place to get laid. But the more successful guys were targets and they knew it. Some of them toured with their wives. They were very discreet about the women."

"I guess I'm a dirty old woman," Patrice said, "but I'm thinking you got some attention from those ladies."

He looked at her sideways. "There's nothing dirty or old about you, madam," he said with some solemnity. "Me, no. Not none, but not a lot. By the time a groupie or some young thing from Scarsdale who thought she wanted to be one was turned down by the singer, then the guitar player, then the bass player and drummer, probably in that order, then the road crew and then anyone else who looked like they might be connected with the act, I was the dregs. And, rude as it may be to say, there was probably a reason the guitar tech turned her down. And for sure way too young."

"Ah," she said. "Sorry to hear it."

"Don't be," he said. "Not my style, anyway. Raised a good Catholic boy. Well, pretty good." He chuckled. "I wasn't entirely immune to temptation, especially when the dope smoke was thick. And I was better-looking then, and in better shape, which is not a big stretch."

"Come on, now . . . ."

"For a couple of years I had an off and on thing going with a supersharp A&R executive for one of the big labels. She was . . . we were . . . ah, it's not so interesting. Toward the end it was mostly off. She was traveling more with the big acts, I worked nights and sometimes traveled with the acts myself. Just hard. Just hard. Ended friendly."

That's what Patrice wanted to hear. Did he know she was fishing? *Is he interested in my love life? Anything about me? Single woman living in The Majestic, he's probably got me figured about right. And he's not the type to pry.*

"My husband passed a few years ago," she said.

"I'm so sorry," Leo said.

"Thank you," she said. "Since then it's been me and Beatrice. Walks in the park, hoping to snap an urban Bigfoot" – Leo chuckled when she raised her camera – "keeping up with friends, keeping an eye on the investments my husband left me. A couple of charity boards, which basically means hitting up friends for tickets to functions no one much wants to attend for causes we'd all rather not think about." She thought it sounded pretty dull as she said it. It struck her that it *was* pretty dull. It sounded somehow small next to Leo's adventures.

So she was surprised when he said, in a voice so oddly dreamy from this rough man, "That sounds like a wonderful life. Time to do the things you want to do, time to work for good causes, lots of friends, and when you relax from all that, a fabulous view from your fabulous home. The greatest city in the world at your feet. Your health. And Beatrice, of course. A reason to wake up every morning."

Yes, Patrice thought. He's right. I should be grateful for what I have and what it lets me do. I can do more.

But as she felt comforted by Leo's reaction, the feeling rose in her that, financially advantaged as she was by her husband's unexpected departure, she was lonely there in her fabulous unit in her fabulous building living the fabulous life this interesting stranger had imagined for her.

She wondered if Leo was going to ask her out, suggest lunch or a drink. He was a talker and obviously a man of action. But his conversation was edged with shyness; he looked elsewhere as he spoke, only occasionally glancing into her eyes. A bodyguard with a nest egg, spent his life being tough, not much practice being charming.

"You didn't seem worried about cops with those kids," Patrice said.

Leo smiled.

"You know all the cops," she said.

"Not all," he said. "But I probably know cops that cops I don't know would know, at least in Manhattan."

"I think I got that."

The pedestrian traffic on the sidewalk before them had increased with midtown workers walking to their apartments on the West Side, their work day done.

"We're starting to lose the light," he said, "getting chilly."

"Yes," she said, "Beatrice and I should be getting back."

"I actually found a parking spot about a half-block from The Majestic," Leo said. "May Warren and I escort you and Beatrice that far?"

Patrice said, "I was going to ask you if you would mind doing just that."

"Be happy to do so."

"One never knows when one might encounter a poodlephobic punk," she said.

Leo laughed a warm gruff laugh. "Warren," he said, "can you walk nicely with Beatrice?"

"I'd worry more about her," Patrice said. "She's been known to nip at smaller dogs."

They walked down Central Park West south toward The Majestic. Patrice had decided she would see Leo again if he asked. The punk episode was a little scary but she realized she had felt secure as he managed the situation. And more than a little entertained. A little like a queen with a champion. No harm done, and a lesson for the punks. There was that roughness and maybe even some hair-trigger unpredictability; but also an old-fashioned courtliness and humor. Apparently he was well-enough off.

She was encouraged that Leo had started things by asking to walk them back and she'd responded as positively as she dared without suggesting he and Warren stop up at the apartment for a cocktail. Now, though, he'd grown quiet as they walked, the dogs out ahead, Beatrice strolling and Warren trotting alongside and looking up at the tall poodle from time to time, and from time to time back at Leo.

"Say," Leo said.

Here it comes, she thought.

"That was some nice camera work, getting their attention with the one flash, and then the second flash to get the picture."

"The D810 has that built-in flash," she said. "I'm just glad it recycled so quickly and there was enough light for autofocus."

"Don't delete that," he said.

As they approached 72nd Street, Leo slowed. He stopped next to a white Bentley convertible with the top down, tan upholstery. Some autumn leaves had decorated the interior. He tossed the skateboard corpse onto the floor of the back seat.

He said, "Thanks for letting Warren and me spend a little of the afternoon with you and Beatrice. Again, sorry for the excitement."

"Don't apologize," she said. "When it was over I realized I had been appreciating the excitement."

"Should have let it go, maybe."

"This is yours?" she said. Her husband had talked about getting something like the Bentley. The quarter-million tag was too much even for him.

"Yeah," he said. "My craziest toy."

Patrice said, "I'm too old to worry about prying. You have to tell me the rest of the story."

Leo laughed. It came out harshly, which he again realized too late, and he ended it with a throat-clear and a chuckle.

"When I graduated from Columbia, it was a huge deal in my family. I was the only college guy ever among all my sibs and cousins. And it was an Ivy, and it was outside of Jersey. Big deal. Really big deal. When I graduated my Uncle Anthony from Queens told me he'd give me $50,000 if I promised not to blow it and to get what he called a 'legitimate' job, which he never really explained, but the implication was that maybe the uncles had made some sketchy but profitable career choices way back when. That was a lot of money from a guy in the waste collection business, so yeah, maybe the garbage business was a little shady. Tony Soprano had the Jersey sanitation business, remember that? Anyway, I bought a used VW Rabbit and thirty shares of Berkshire Hathaway."

"Smart," she said.

"Lucky," he said. "But the capital gain takes some of the edge off."

"Still."

"Uncle Anthony is no longer with us," Leo said, "so I'm blowing it now."

There didn't seem to be much more to say.

"We're only a half-block from your lobby," Leo said.

"We'll be fine the rest of the way." Patrice had had enough of waiting for this guy to make a move. "I can't believe how Beatrice is getting along with Warren," she said. "She's not exactly a dog who likes dogs, but look at them."

The dogs weren't doing anything other than standing and panting and looking expectantly at their respective owners.

"Quite a pack," Leo said.

Patrice thought back to Leo's gift of gallantry. He had not just defended the honor of a dog who could not have cared less. He instantly recognized the insult to Patrice herself. He didn't like the threat to gay men who were nowhere nearby. He had values. It was like he felt the danger to civilization from too many acts of uncivilized behavior by ignorant people gone unchallenged and would stand against at least this one.

She saw how he worked to tamp down the apprehension people could feel around him, sensing his power and readiness to act. His fine clothes, his careful locution, the muted gravel of his voice. His little dog.

He was a man of substance.

She realized she was touched, touched deeply by this man's man, muscle and courage and action and brains, all wrapped around a fragile core of loneliness. How long had it taken him to decide to walk up to her and say *Your dog is beautiful?* She was glad she had muted her own instinct to brush off this Central Park stranger.

He was a nice man.

She would see him again.

The thought thrilled her.

"You ever do a doggie play date with Warren?" she asked. "Get Warren together with another dog for dog stuff, chasing and playing and whatever, some permitted butt-sniffing?"

"A doggie play date," Leo mused. "I never have."

"Week from today, let's do it a little earlier when it's warmer, say one o'clock. Meet us at the bench. I'll pack some sandwiches and drinks. You good with tuna, turkey, the usual?"

He didn't have long to consider that she wasn't inviting him and Warren to a doggie date, she had already scheduled it and booked his acceptance. He'd never experienced this type of interest from a woman of this one's style and class and decided instantly that it suited him.

"Yeah, love 'em, but that's a lot of trouble. Why don't I just stop at a deli and pick us up some –"

"Nope nope nope," Patrice said. "I make a special tuna salad you're gonna love. I want to do it. Slap it on some amazing rye from Fine & Shapiro – you don't have a gluten issue, do you? Just load up Warren and meet me and Beatrice."

"Can't I contribute something to the cause here?"

"Well, we're not supposed to drink in the Park," she said, "but I've got a couple of fake soda cans made for occasions just like this. Maybe some wine that goes with Milk Bones. Make sure it's a screw-top in some kind of non-winey bag. We get busted, we'll move our operation." She jerked her head – a slight and ladylike jerk – at the looming Majestic a half-block away. She got into her wallet and pulled out an old calling card she'd had printed up years before with her name and number on it. "Call me if something comes up."

"If weather permits," Leo said.

"It wouldn't dare not," Patrice said.

Leo looked at the card and stroked its frayed corners.

"Or just call sometime," she said. "If you feel like it."

He lifted Warren into the Bentley, then reached out to Patrice. She held out her hand and he took her slim well-tended fingers in his knotted rough ones. He lifted her hand a little, like he was considering kissing it, but did not. He held her hand with exquisite gentleness and let his thumb rest almost imperceptibly across its back, drawing it lightly across her skin as they parted.

"I'll bring the poop bags," he said.

5

LEO WATCHED THE tall cool woman and dog glide south and cross the street.

Good dog, Warren.

The Mom and the Man

1

"HEY," ALLISON SAID as the girl let the door to the kitchen slam behind her. "How was school? Don't slam the door."

"Same as always," Carly said. She shrugged off her backpack and opened the refrigerator door. She gazed into it and sighed that early-teen girlsigh, consumed with tragic resignation that there was nothing in there she wanted. "Boring, hard, most of the kids suck, except for my friends, and even some of them sometimes."

"Don't forget to complain about homework."

"I'd like to forget everything about homework. But I won't."

"Don't forget to complain about how you'll never use any of the stuff they're teaching."

"I haven't forgotten," Carly said, "but I've heard your lecture on that like a million times."

"And don't say 'suck,'" Allison said.

"Stink."

"Better."

"Everyone says 'sucks,'" Carly said.

Allison thought about how language changes over the

years. *Sucks. Blows.* Maybe kids didn't associate those words with fellatio anymore. *Precocious* applied to a child used to mean *intelligent beyond a child's years*; now it means *uncomfortably sexually oversophisticated and smart-mouthed.*

"I don't understand how you can not like school," she said. "So much cool stuff to learn, great books to read, friends you will have your whole life. Cheering for the team, tons of activities, clubs for all kinds of interests. Middle school's kind of a rough time for boys and girls your age, I appreciate that. I had to go through that whole girl-body-changey thing, but you'll get through it and you're going to love high school."

Carly hoisted herself onto one of the stools lined up along the kitchen island and considered whether it would hurt her to eat the apple she'd grabbed from the basket of fruit Allison kept out. "That's like a million years from now."

"One more year."

"Dumb boys, dumb girls, dumb teachers –"

Allison looked up from chopping vegetables for their salad.

"I'm sorry," Carly said. "I didn't mean you. You're smart."

"Thank you," Allison said. "I'm smart about world literature."

"But yeah, you're really smart! School was easy for you!"

"You think life is unfair? Well let me tell you something. I wasn't that smart. But thank God, I was cute. Really cute. That didn't help me with grades – well, maybe once. Maybe twice. But it made everything easier for me outside the classroom and so I could concentrate on getting the grades. And you're even cuter than I was. You're lovely, Carly, you'll be popular in high school and that will be fun. Not fair, maybe, but fun. And you can focus on learning like I did."

"Mom." Carly rolled her eyes. "I'm not. Compared to some of the girls who –" She pantomimed breasts.

"You are. You know it. I'll bet you're starting to hear it, too. Don't worry about the . . . development. We're going to have a little talk one of these days."

"Mom, we had that talk a million years ago."

"Different talk. About boys. About growing boys. But my point is that there are lots of girls, boys too, who are not cute, some are the opposite of cute, and think what school is like for them, and then sometimes even life. It's not fair, but it's the way it is, that's the way the whole world works sometimes. I don't make the rules. I hope you are nice to everyone no matter what they look like."

"I am," Carly said. "Some of the girls aren't."

"You stay away from the mean girls."

"I will. I do."

Allison said, "You got me off the subject. You are plenty smart, sharp and quick like your father, you soak stuff up fast so let's have no woe-is-me talk about school. Even stuff you think you'll never need when you're older. It makes –"

"No!" Carly said. "Please, I *get* it. Well-rounded, learning how to think, gotta know about the *world*, blah-blah, I *get* it! Not the lecture, please!"

"Okay, all right," Allison said. "Just remember that looks only take you so far. And for so long."

"I never thought they'd take me anywhere. I still don't."

"There'll come a time," Allison said. "You'll be glad you had the looks but you'll be even gladder you have the grades and the degrees." She frowned quizzically. "Gladder?

More glad? Whatever, you'll be it." She shook her head and returned her concentration to dinner preparation.

"Mom, you're still cute. I mean, you're beautiful."

"Oh. Oh!" Allison felt a tear coming on and she turned her head from the onion slices. "Thank you, Carly, that's very sweet."

"I mean it. Dad must have been crazy to – you know, whatever."

Allison said, "We're not going to talk bad about your father. He could limber up his check-signing hand a little more regularly, but we're doing okay, aren't we?"

"*Are* we?" Carly said, with that teengirl staginess.

"Yes, we *are*," Allison mocked back. "You and me, we're doing great."

Carly slid off the stool and stared at her mother.

"What?" Allison said. "What? Why are you –"

"A man moved into the Felders' house."

"What?"

"A man."

"I saw the 'sold' sign," Allison said. She had seen more than that. "Well, that's good. Don't like to have neighborhood houses empty."

"Just a man."

"What do you mean, 'just a man'?"

"I mean I didn't see any kids or a woman or anything."

"They could be coming later."

"He's been there a few days," Carly said. "He's been working around the outside, planting stuff, painting some trim. Two cars. Well, a cool sporty car and one of those big SUVs, but he's the only one driving them."

"I hope you haven't been spying on him."

"Nope, just see him when I'm coming or going."

"Did you talk to him?"

"Nope. But he saw me looking at him when he was getting his mail when Ms. Ainsley dropped me off after Pep Club. And you know what he did? He saw me looking at him and he tipped his hat to me! It was kind of a straw hat, and he touched the front of it with two fingers, kind of bent it down a little, and he bowed his head toward me a little. And he smiled and then he gave just a little wave. It was *so cool!*"

"We're definitely going to have that talk," Allison said.

"He wasn't being weird or anything," Carly said.

"I guess it isn't so odd for a single man to have a whole house to himself," Allison said.

"He's cute," Carly said. "Handsome."

"Carly."

"I think you should take him some cookies or a cake or something, a little goody package, welcome to the neighbs. Maybe a bottle of wine."

"Carly!"

"I know you're lonely."

"Carly!"

"And you're hot. And all your hotness is just going to waste sitting around here or teaching high school kids Shakespeare or whatever and you should be dating."

"Maybe someday, daughter," she said. "Not just now."

"Just when? You're like at peak hotness!"

"I don't feel hot," Allison said. "I feel tired. I still need to think about why things went the way they did with your father, why things changed for him, for the two of us. And everything has changed, the online stuff, dating . . . ."

And what do you do about intimacy with a knows-everything daughter in the house?

"You tell me not to make excuses," Carly said. "He's not online, he's like right in our front yard! I'm not saying you have to have – I'm not saying you have to fall in love with him, I'm just saying to meet him."

Allison said, "I don't know what to do with my hair. Grey, look." She bent down to her daughter and parted her hair with her hands.

"Mom! It's like nothing! I'm seeing maybe three hairs," Carly said. "And women color their hair, you know, and do all kinds of other things to keep the hotness going. Your hair is cute enough, but maybe . . . ."

"And my upper arms! Look at these saggy things!"

"Mom!" Carly said, "Guys don't care anything about your upper arms. You have a great butt, and your boobs –"

"Carly, I mean really!"

"You're the one who's running yourself down," she said. "I'm just saying you still look like Miss Cincinnati to me and to guys too." *It was a mistake to let her look through that old album*, Allison thought. "You know guys check you out when you're leaning over squeezing the avocados at Kroger."

"I know nothing of the sort," Allison said.

"A million kids ask me if Ms. Sanders at the high school is my mom. Mostly boys. You're famous."

"How do you know if I'm lonely?" Allison said.

Carly gave Allison a look with a fist on a cocked hip that said *Mother*.

"All right," Allison said. "Hey, is this about you wanting to date? 'If Mom does, then I can too'? You're still thirteen, my dear."

"Can't I just want you to be happy?"

"Oh, Carly Ann," she said. "I suppose so."

"And I'm fourteen month after next. Mom, I'd be totally cool with a stepdad. Some girls at school have 'em. They say they got to be in a cool wedding and their house is happy again because their mom is happy and the new dad bends over backwards to make them like him. And the old dad takes them places and gets them stuff because he wants them to still like him."

"Let's not get ahead of ourselves with the 'new dad' business. And that 'old dad' is actually 'Dad,' remember that."

"OO! OO! You could have a baby! Ms. Allen was forty-three when she had Lars!"

Allison shook her head and laughed. "Okay, missy, now you're getting crazy. You think I want another teenager to deal with when I'm pushing fifty? Wait, how did you know she was forty-three?"

"He usually comes home around 5:45," Carly said, biting into the apple. "First thing he does is check the mailbox."

Allison sighed. "I know."

2

"I'M CARLY SANDERS."

"Well, hello, Carly Sanders. My name is Roger Housman. Nice to meet you. Thanks for coming over to say hi." He held out his hand and Carly shook it. "I guess I should get around and meet some of the neighbors." He flipped through the mail he'd taken from the box. "Just checking the daily junk delivery."

"My mom is Allison Sanders. We live in that house."
She pointed.

"Yes," he said. "I saw you come home the other day."

"Oh, yeah," she giggled.

"What grade are you in?"

"Seventh, at the middle school. My mom teaches
English at the high school."

"That's excellent," he said. "I loved English in school.
I wish I had more time to read now. What's your favorite subject?"

"I guess I don't have one," she said. "Anything except
science."

"Oh," he said, "you gotta love science. Math, too. That's
the way the world's going. It may be hard to get into but
once you do, you'll want to learn more and more. And we
need more girls getting interested in those areas."

"Yeah, I know," Carly said. "They tell us that all the
time. I guess I my head isn't right for it."

"I promise you it absolutely is," Roger said. "Don't let
the boys have all the fun and invent all the cool stuff and
make all the money."

"Anyway, I just wanted to say hi and welcome to the
neighborhood. So welcome to the neighborhood! My mom
Allison is probably going crazy watching us thinking I'm
bothering you."

Roger laughed. "You can tell her I said you weren't.
Coming over to introduce yourself was a very civilized and
mature thing to do. Your mother has obviously raised you
right."

"She's a great mom," Carly said. "She's really cool, and
she's – . Well, you really should meet her sometime."

Roger smiled and said, "If she's as friendly as you are I'm sure we will meet soon."

"She's real friendly," Carly said. "Super nice. You'll like her. It's just her and me. Her name is Allison."

"So you said. Allison Sanders. Got it."

3

"CARLY SANDERS! WHAT were you saying to him? I saw you look back over here!"

"I just said hello and introduced myself," Carly said. "And I told him your name. His name is Roger Housman."

"Oh my god," Allison said.

"Don't worry, it was cool," Carly said. "It's not like I told him you were hot and looking for a man or anything. He was very nice, he asked me about school and stuff."

"Oh my god."

"Mom, I had to! I saw Ms. Beeman talking to him the other day in that swimsuit and coverup thing she wears all the time that shows off her stuff. She doesn't even have a pool and I don't think her jacuzzi even works. She's flirting all the time with the FedEx and Amazon guys when they come by. This was ten times worse! You need to meet him."

"I'm sure I'll meet him sometime. Please don't bother the poor man."

"I told him you'd say that. He said to tell you I wasn't bothering him."

"You've introduced yourself, and me too, I guess, now leave him alone."

Carly snorted and flounced. "There are two other single women on this street and you know Ms. Akers is going to find some way to swing around the cul-de-sac in her hot little Mustang convertible. And probably a ton more in the subdivision who know a cute single guy has moved in. Come on! You need to get out there."

"What else did you tell him?"

"I told him you were super nice and friendly."

"Oh my god, you've probably got him thinking I'm a hooker. What else? You didn't tell him about Miss Cincinnati!"

"No," Carly said, filing away that thought for a possible future encounter with Mr. Housman. "I told him you taught at the high school."

"Well, that's okay."

"And I told him it was just you and me."

"Oh, I'm sure he was able to decipher your little hints that mom was not married," Allison said.

"And I told him you were a great mom."

"Oh, Carly," Allison said, a tiny lump of pride rising to nudge some mist into her eyes. *She knows how to push my buttons and I am a complete sucker for it.* "Look, my sweet baby girl, I appreciate your concern and you wanting to jump-start my romantic life, but I didn't just fall off the banana boat, you know."

"You need to get off the banana boat," Carly said. "I know about bananas, and they won't put a ring on your finger."

"CARLY ANN! What do you mean you know about banan – never mind. Oh my god, society shouldn't let teenaged girls talk to each other."

"What's that book?" Carly said. It looked like an old-fashioned three-ring binder with a lot of tabs.

Allison had been turning pages as they spoke, and she

turned a couple more. "What do you think? Chocolate chip, peanut butter, oatmeal?"

Carly brightened. "Mom, great! You've been totally faking me out! Maybe some of each? I'll help! I'll make them while you go doll out! I'll help you pick out a cute outfit while they're in the oven. Ooo, we need to pick a wine that goes with cookies!"

"Whoa," Allison said. "Too late today, and I don't know if I have everything I need."

"Tomorrow, Saturday, perfect," Carly said. "After we get what you need for the cookies we'll go to Nordy's for some cute shoes. I'm picturing an outfit."

"Picture digging into that astronomy unit you were complaining about," Allison said. "You need to get those science and math grades up to get into high school AP if you're thinking about an Ivy."

"You're the one thinking about an Ivy," she said. She raised her arms in the air. "Go Buckeyes!"

"Buckeyes need to know astronomy, too," Allison said. "I can dress myself for a visit to Mr. Housman."

"You can but you won't," Carly said. "Cookies just get you in the door. Legs, butt, boobs, gotta sell it, Mom."

"Stop with the boobs and butt! You make him sound totally superficial," Allison said. "Besides, you just said men already check me out at the grocery store while I'm squeezing avocados."

"You've never seen yourself leaning over the avocado bin to squeeze the ones at the back. The produce kid's voice changed."

"What do you know about boys' voices chan – no, no, I don't want to know," Allison said.

"Alls I'm saying is you got . . . features. You don't have to look slutty –"

"Carly!"

"— just use them a little, don't hide them."

"You don't want your mother to look cheap."

"Gotta get his attention first, then find out if he's a jerk or cool. Come on, at least show off your legs."

"Astro unit," Allison said. "Get going."

"We'll need to work on your hair," Carly said.

4

ALLISON HAD TO admit: her hair looked good. Cute, Carly said. Okay, it looked cute.

Where did young teenaged girls learn about hair and makeup and clothes? Slumber parties? Magazines? As a beauty contestant when she was a girl Allison always had older women and pageant experts putting her together, and she carried those lessons into adulthood. Perhaps held on to those old lessons for too long. Maybe Carly was right – she needed to freshen up her look, get with the times, sex things up a little.

Sex. Is that why she was standing at the front door of Mr. Roger Housman?

No.

No.

Oh . . . yes, it was part of the suite of benefits and emotions and . . . stuff, feelings, that accompanied a relationship with a man. But it was only a part, a rather small part, actually, temporally speaking. Yes, a very nice part. But still, a part, one that goes along with having someone to talk to and listen to, someone to laugh with, someone who supports you and whom you support, someone to tell you not to worry about that noise you heard after lights-out, someone to do things with. Someone to be next to you when people look at you and think *they're a couple* that you are proud for people to think even in this day of gender-muted pairings. Someone to assemble unassembled things. Someone to smile at you for no reason, or maybe for a reason you gave him. Someone to put his hands on your waist from behind while you're stirring the meat sauce and breathe in your unwashed hair like it was the mane of a chocolate unicorn.

Yes, maybe a little lonely.

Carly had won the battle of the legs and the butt. Allison was wearing white cuffed shorts, a little below mid-thigh and loose at the cuff but snug as they traveled north. Strappy heeled sandals that tensed and elevated her long calves and kept her glutes at attention. Her stretchy tube top permitted the very slightest glimpse of cleavage, and it was covered with a crisp ice-yellow cotton top, unbuttoned.

Everything tasteful, appropriate for late spring, but playful in a civilized way for calling on a single man of potential intrigue.

She had seen him for just a few minutes at a time from her kitchen window. He was three doors down at the end of their cul-de-sac and she couldn't see much, but she liked the way he moved and what she could tell of his size and shape and hair. What was that phrase? – she liked the cut of his jib. Allison didn't know what a jib was, but at least from a three-doors-down distance, whatever it was seemed to be cut in a very appealing way. Carly thought he was cute and handsome, and, much as Allison hated to admit it, at thirteen her girl had an eye.

She carried with her a plate of chocolate chip and oatmeal cookies, and a Santa Barbara pinot grigio that was pretty nice, she thought. She had figured a price halfway between the cheapest and most expensive bottles at Kroger, added five bucks, and bought the first white she saw at that price.

But now that she was standing there on his porch, she wasn't sure . . . .

What am I doing here? Am I here to flirt? Am I here to be a good neighbor? Am I here just to practice my man-chops for when I'm really ready to date again? Am I here because Carly has nagged me into it and because I need to make sure she hasn't bugged the man to death?

Don't lie to yourself, Allison: I'm here because I've seen this guy a few times puttering around his yard or going or coming and I kept watching. I'm here because if he can afford this house and drive a Land Rover and that little Jaguar F-something, then he's some kind of responsible citizen.

The old feelings coming back.

I told Carly this was no big deal but she didn't believe a word because I let her consult on my hair and help put together my look from what we mined from my tired closet and make sure my makeup was up to date and the whole thing was girly fun and it took us over an hour.

And after all that I look good. And I like that feeling of looking good and men looking at me and thinking so, too. And he will. He will. And I'm looking forward to liking that feeling, even if he's not it. So, even if it's only that feeling . . . . Yes, even if.

She rang the doorbell.

Roger Housman was tall and broad. He was wearing a white oxford button-down shirt, buttoned-down, tucked in to faded, but not too faded, jeans cinched up with a hemp belt. He stood in some beat-up, but not too beat-up, boots. The face she could only guess at from three doors down turned out to be smooth, warm, bemused. Friendly, but immediately observant, taking her in in an appraising but non-threatening way. Carly had said *cute* and *handsome*. Not the same thing, necessarily, but he was both. She guessed mid- to late-thirties. She could work with that, with all of it, in fact. He appeared comfortable in his studied-rumpled clothes – but not too studied or too rumpled.

He looked at the cookies and wine and smiled.

"Hi," she said, "I'm Allison Sanders from 8941, the tan brick? I think you've met my daughter Carly."

"I sure have," he said. "Carly is charming. Please come in. I'm Roger Housman."

Her hands were full so no handshake. "She can be a bit of a pest."

"Perhaps, but not with me. It was sweet of her to say hello."

He took the plate of cookies and wine from her. "I hope you like either chocolate chip or oatmeal," she said. "I know it's quite a lot of cookies but I wasn't sure . . . ."

"Just me," he said, "but I'm still stocking my snack larder so I'll definitely polish these off before too long."

"And the wine, I just guessed."

"Can't go wrong with pinot grigio. This is a cool-looking label, look at all those pastel orchids. Having a label with lots of colors is the only way I know how to judge wine, so I'm sure this is excellent."

He made a short trip to the kitchen to put the wine in the refrigerator.

"My manners!" he said. "Won't you please sit for a bit?"

"Perhaps for a bit," Allison said. "Thank you."

Where to sit? The family room had a long couch and a couple of chairs. Nice stuff. What message would it send if she sat on the couch? Too forward? Too distant and timid if she sat in one of the chairs?

She sat at the end of the couch.

He sat at the other end.

She canted herself towards him and crossed her long legs. Carly was right about the legs. You can show them off without being too cheap, and she still had those lean dancer's stems.

"I was serious," Roger said, "Carly is a sweetie. And she's a big fan of yours. I've never raised a teenaged daughter but I understand those can be difficult years between mother and daughter."

"Oh, we have our issues," Allison said. "You say you've never raised a teenaged daughter . . . ."

"Or son, either," Roger said.

"I didn't mean to pry." *The hell.*

"I'm sure the neighborhood is curious about the single man who bought the big house. I don't mind, I'd be curious myself. I think it's good to be at least a little informed about your neighbors. These days we should make an effort not to be so isolated. I'll give you a quick download and you can tell anyone you want."

"Really, Roger, I didn't come over here to be nosy."

The hell, again. She called him *Roger.* It gave her a little thrill. On top of the thrill of lying about not coming over to be nosy.

"No, really, Allison, I don't want to bore you but you came over here to introduce yourself so I'd better introduce myself back, and then I'll want to hear about you and Carly, too." He said her name, *Allison,* and she liked that sound, too, then he said it again: "I should ask: Do you go by Allison? Ally?"

"Allison," she said. "'Ally' always sounded kind of . . . cattish to me."

He laughed. "I like the name *Allison,*" he said. "It's very . . . very . . . sophisticated-sounding. Anyway, yeah. So, how did I get here. I was always a nerd, read everything I could get my hands on as a kid, always liked hanging out at museums, summer jobs there, ended up with a Masters in gallery and museum management. Yeah, they really do have programs for that, they had a good one at Western Colorado. Bummed around on the slopes for a while but got a job at Crosetti Museum in Dayton and worked there for a couple years, then caught on as Curator of Native American Art and Culture at the University museum branch in Lima. I liked that a lot, learned a lot about dealing with academics and donors. Moved into University development; in other words, fundraising. I get the profs to come to cocktail parties with the big donors, talk about their work, show a PowerPoint my staff has helped them polish up. Then I'm the guy who says 'thanks for coming, it takes a lot of money for our great professors to do all the neat stuff you just saw, so please give us some of yours.' People think the money all comes from the football donors, but we raise a surprising amount through the academic programs. I was doing more and more work in development but I was at the Lima campus commuting down here a lot, and they wanted to promote me but said I'd have to move here. They did and I did, so here I am."

"Wow," Allison said. She tried to think of something imaginative, something to keep him talking, but what came out was: "Sounds really interesting."

"It is, very," Roger said. "I left something out."

Marriage? Young kid being raised in a commune somewhere? Prison? Fast zombie?

He went over and pulled a DVD case out of a stack. It was *Startle*. Allison had heard of the movie, some kind of teens-in-the-woods thing except in outer space. Something like that.

Roger said, "One-in-a-million shot. I had this screenplay I'd written after grad school. Just fooling around. I knew this woman bang out of film studies at University of Denver who was crazy to produce and direct something but all she was seeing were these artsy undergrad relationship scripts and moronic frat comedies. I offered her the script for gross points if it made money."

"And it did, didn't it? Kind of a sleeper hit?"

"Yeah," he said, "a sleeper. Let's put it this way – it slept so successfully it lets me work in education, really my first love, and still live well. And Azizi Okafor, it was her first film role so when she hit it big with the Costner thing a few years later, it meant continuing interest in *Startle*, and a check now and then. This probably sounds like bragging –"

"Not at all," Allison said, although it did, a little. He wanted her to know where the money came from. "I'm

impressed. Is this something I could watch with Carly some
—"

"Ah, no," he said. "A little strong for middle-schoolers, some underage alien nudity and inter-entity sex, although these days . . . ."

"Tell me about it," Allison said.

She recrossed her legs.

Allison liked this Roger Housman. She hadn't expected him to be so forthcoming, but she found herself instantly at ease with his own ease at telling his story. She remembered many dates – so many dates – where she'd had to carry the conversational ball because the guy just had nothing. But Roger knew that the neighbors with young families would be curious about a single man moving in, and he wanted everyone to know he was –

Well, what are you, Roger Housman? Very attractive, very smart, very well-off, we can all see that, and yes, we know that people don't rush into marriage these days, and yes, single people can be fulfilled being single and blah-blah-blah, but what IS your story, your real story, the part of your story I'm really interested in? Ha, maybe I'll send Carly over, let her snoop about your love life. Let's try this:

"Carly's actually fairly easy," Allison said. "I know some single moms who are completely outmatched."

"Carly did mention it was just the two of you," Roger said. "Might have let that slip more than once, in fact."

"Miss Carly can be a bit of a busybody."

"She's just looking out for you. That's admirable."

"Her father and I split two years ago. You know those Indian casino ads that tell you to come gamble, and also where to get help with a gambling addiction? He only read the first part. I never really knew why he started . . . . Anyway, I got tired of arguing with him about money, and about what he was doing at the casinos, and he got tired of it too. At least now I know all of my salary is mine and the creditors don't call any more. But he was a good dad, still is. One of those things where we're better friends now than when we were married, at least at the end." She instantly regretted the final remark, and wanted Roger to understand *but not with benefits*.

Roger looked at her, thinking of something. "Would it be appropriate to open that bottle of colorful wine you brought?" he said.

"I think it would," she said.

While he was gone she looked around the room. Very male. Fabulous TV and audio equipment. Quality but plain furniture that didn't quite match, and that clashed a little with the nice Oriental rug. A short stack of books on an end table, each with a bookmark indicating some progress: a book on quantum physics for lay people; some essays by a whiz-kid writer known for his impenetrable novels; two books of short stories by female authors; a contemporary poetry anthology; and – thank God – *I, Sniper* by Stephen Hunter. The thriller on top of the stack, good, and the only one with the bookmark indicating progress more than halfway.

He returned and handed her the glass. They *clinked*, a little awkwardly, to nothing in particular, but in that *clink* was just the tiniest mutual acknowledgment that the conversation had warmed up from a neighborhood welcome to . . . something warmer. Something clinky. Or so it seemed to Allison.

Roger sat back down at the far end of the sofa and smiled, a little sadly, she thought. "I was engaged," he said.

"The movie woman? Oh," Allison said, "I really beg your pardon, your personal life is none of my business." *The hell.*

"It's all right. No, the movie woman, Regina Wood was her name, Google her, she's done some great stuff, she'll have an Oscar someday – different relationship. My fiancée's name was Felicia. We dated a couple of years then got engaged. We were actually engaged for a while. I guess we were a little conservative about making sure we were both established before we got married. She was an interior designer. I regret that now. I've often thought we should have just said the hell with security and let's do it. Anyway, something must have been eating at her because one day I came back from Columbus and she'd been to a religious rally – Timothy Koppel, that TV evangelist, touring the country with his live act – and said she'd been born again and if I wasn't born again we would be unequally yoked, was the way she put it. I tried not to be disrespectful of that position, I truly did."

He stopped, and Allison shook her head and touched her chest, *don't worry, I'm not born again.* "Okay, but I did try to understand. But being born again is apparently something you either are or you aren't and there's no room for compromise and if you are born again then marrying someone bound for hell is not considered a prudent choice. We didn't fight about it. She just said she was sorry for my soul and would pray for me but she didn't seem too optimistic about that as a pre-marital strategy and before too long she broke it off and disappeared into the movement. I lost track of her but wondered what she did when Koppel got busted with the wife of one of his trustees. Whatever it was – my yoke is still empty."

"I'm sorry," Allison said.

"Me too."

"You just never know, do you?"

"I sure didn't."

"That may have been the dumbest thing I have ever said," she laughed.

"Well," he said, "if you're going to lose your woman to someone, I guess you can't feel too bad if it's Jesus."

Allison laughed. Roger Housman didn't take himself too seriously.

Carly must be doing handstands that I haven't returned yet. Old Mom has transformed cookies into a little date here. Allison was glad she had taken care of her legs and kept that old underwire strapless bra she had been thinking of throwing away. She recrossed her legs again.

"Your turn," he said. "I loved that Carly said you teach English at the high school. Do tell."

"That's right. English, all three grades."

"What's on the syllabus these days?"

"It's changed since I started teaching. Much more world literature, much more Black and Hispanic literature. Women writers. But god, so much sex in the newer stuff, we have to be careful. Bad language. We still teach Shakespeare, *Huckleberry Finn*, a Brontë here and there, Jane Austen. *Lord of the Flies*, the old standby. Faulkner and Salinger for the AP classes. Major poets. At least one black writer per year, usually Morrison or Ellison, and maybe a Latino magical realist. Short story specialists like Poe, Hemingway. Fitzgerald. I still like the dead white drunks, sorry."

"No need to apologize to me," Roger said. "So much wonderful stuff," Roger said. "I don't know how you fit it all in."

"I was admiring your stack here."

"Oh. Yeah. I try to keep a bunch of stuff going at once. That pile isn't as daunting as it may look. I used to feel a moral obligation to finish every book I started, but as the years have gone by I value my time more dearly, so if a book sucks – pardon my language – or if it's too far over my head I put it aside."

He thinks "sucks" is vulgar. I need to tell Carly. He doesn't waste his time with junk. Me neither.

"Are kids excited by great writing, great literature, these days?" he asked.

"Like everything else. Mixed bag. Some of the dreamy kids, the smarter kids, the lifelong readers love it, like you and I probably do, for the beauty of the language, the insight into the human condition. And, let's face it, the great storytelling, right?"

"Oh, absolutely."

"And then there are some who think even the best literature is completely useless, won't make them any money, takes them away from their games. And of course, there are the kids who find insults and prejudice and oppression in everything, or pretend to. The parents are worse. I'm surprised they're not demanding *Moby Dick* be removed from the curriculum because the whale is white."

"And yet . . . ," Roger smiled.

"And yet," she said, "I love it. It's worth it if you can see the light go on in just a few kids every year. And overall, I have to say, by the time graduation rolls around, most everyone is tolerable. They'll be all right."

Roger brought the bottle and refilled their glasses. "The students I have contact with at the University tend to be those who already get it," he said. "Grad students, the brighter undergrads, the ones we show off to donors. Funny, isn't it," he said, "each generation seems like it's going to hell and yet you stand back and poof, you see progress everywhere you look if you just let yourself. The background noise from social media, the idiots who used to be edited out of what we read and watched, drown out the good."

Exactly what I was telling a vice-principal the other day.
I need to watch this wine.
Roger Housman an interesting man.
He's nice. He's smart. He looks good.
And if he's not lying he's heterosexual and not weird.
That Carly.

"Be honest with you," he said, "I'm taking a little break from reading. Those bookmarks have not moved in a while, except maybe the sniper novel. I finished *Middlemarch* a couple of weeks back, eight hundred pages –"

Allison sat up a little straighter. "No! You did not read *Middlemarch*!"

"I didn't?" Roger said. "I wonder what was on those eight hundred pages."

"No, sorry," Allison laughed. "I mean – that's my favorite novel of all time. Really."

"It was amazing," he said. "I know Jane Austen is *de rigueur* these days, but I just could not get through *Mansfield*

Park, put it aside about a third through. *Middlemarch*, though – a woman writing about a woman – really, women – really, men and women – who engage with the issues that engage us today. But the thing of it was, I was absolutely transfixed by the beauty of Eliot's prose. Those long, lyrical sentences that for all their complexity were quite clear, carried me right along. Stand aside, Hemingway and Elmore Leonard and Ann Beattie."

"Yes," Allison said. "Yes." Was this happening? She was sitting with an age-appropriate handsome man who lived three doors from her and had comfortably referenced Austen, Eliot, Hemingway, Leonard, and Beattie, and had all his hair and a Jaguar and liked women and wrote a movie with alien sex.

He said, "I would be interested in your reaction to my impression that her writing seemed oddly modern, even if somewhat ornate to today's ears."

"Yes," she said. "Isn't it amazing? I like Hemingway and Leonard too but the observations she packs into her sentences! In a way, it's thrilling to read, you forget you're reading a huge novel. Like Tolstoy."

"*War and Peace* is on my list," he said. "I figured if I could get through David Foster Wallace . . . ."

"You didn't read *Infinite Jest*," she said.

"Finished it last summer," Roger said. "Footnotes and all." He pointed to a bookshelf next to the television. There it was, the paperback binding wrinkled from many openings.

Allison knew this was not some kind of fake intellectual flirtation. He would have no way of knowing of her love of George Eliot or that she was the only person she knew who had actually read *Infinite Jest* instead of just having claimed to have read it.

This sit-down was too perfect. It was going way too well. The mystery wine was actually good. Too good. She had to regroup, to think over what she had seen and heard with this man before she said something to screw the whole thing up, if there was even a whole thing to screw up.

"Well," Allison said, "I certainly did not intend to take up so much of your time today."

"I'm glad you did," he said. "It's not every day a guy is just sitting around trying to think of something to do and Miss Cincinnati rings his doorbell with sweets and alcohol and a love of George Eliot."

"Carly said she hadn't told you!" Allison said. "Oh, that girl is so grounded," although there wasn't anywhere Carly was able to go in any event.

"Carly did not tell me."

"So how did you know? That was sixteen years ago. I was a senior in high school. I'm sure you didn't recognize me."

He laughed. "You step outdoors from time to time yourself, and this house has windows, too. Forgive me for being a man, but the truth is that I was able to identify you as the mother of whom Carly thought so highly and who seemed so anxious for me to meet. And I thought, if I might be so bold, I thought 'hmm, that would not be such an awful thing, to meet Carly's mom.'"

"You saw me, and . . . ."

"And the internet has uses besides social media."

"So you Googled me. Wait, my name wasn't Sanders in those days, so . . . ."

"So I surmised you were divorced. Your divorce papers were online and not sealed, and your maiden name was in them. Allison Rockheim is not a common name, so you were a pretty quick lookup. Hey, look, I'm sorry, I certainly didn't mean to embarrass you and I'm not a stalker. It was just an interesting fact about you. And it is also interesting that you haven't mentioned it or hinted at it in a round-about way as a lot of women would have. A very becoming modesty. I'm not one of these people who makes fun of beauty queens. I admire the determination and self-confidence it must take."

Allison hadn't liked all the folderol that went along with the pageant life, and she'd had to be alert to sense the kind of guys who just wanted to get with the pageant girls because they were the pageant girls. But she had liked the attention and she had liked the winning and she had liked being beautiful and she was fearful of the passage of time and the day she would not turn heads.

But that day is not here yet, dammit. This man is in my wheelhouse and I'm in his.

"It was a long time ago."

"What was your talent, if I may ask?"

"Oh, god," she said. "Talk about dating myself. I came out dressed and wigged and eyelashed and made up and all busty like Loni Anderson and belted out the theme song to 'WKRP in Cincinnati.' I had a little choreography to go along with it since the song is short. Wrote some extra lyrics to stretch it some, some stuff about how great Cincinnati is. Then, before the final phrase, I stopped the music, stared right at the judges and said: 'As God is my witness, I thought turkeys could fly.' Then big vocal finish.

The auditorium went absolutely bonkers, literally screaming for me. I wasn't the prettiest girl there, but after that the
judges couldn't deny a true daughter of their fair city, and
they wanted to get out of there alive."

Roger had started laughing halfway through her
account. "I'm majorly doubting you weren't the prettiest.
I would love to know all about it, what happened after,
I guess you went on to the Miss Ohio pageant? Do you
mind talking about it? It's really an extraordinary thing to
do in one's life. Perhaps another time if you feel you need
to get back."

"I don't mind talking about it but perhaps" – *oh, god,
am I about to suggest another get-together? Didn't he just suggest it? This wine* – "another time."

"Sure. I'm sorry if I made you uncomfortable, spring-
ing that on you."

"No. No, you didn't. I'm choosing to be flattered,"
she said.

Roger smiled as they stood.

"You should," he said.

5

"Mom! You've been gone forEVer! Was he cool? He was,
wasn't he? And cute, wasn't he? I *told* you! Mom! Are you
in love?"

Allison turned to her daughter, a little glazed, as though
she hadn't heard her right away.

"That's not as crazy a question as it sounds," she said.

6

"MOM'S NOT HOME," Carly said. "Ooo, I'm so sorry." She really was. "Do you want to come in? I'm sure she won't be long. I'll text her."

"No no," Roger said. "I'm just returning her cookie platter. All washed and shiny."

Good move, Mom.

"Oh. Thanks."

"Tell your mom the cookies were delicious," he said. "And tell her thanks again."

"I did the oatmeal."

"Well then, I'll tell you: the cookies were delicious. Also, I had meant to give her my contact information in case you ladies need something over here that requires a little male elbow grease." He handed her a university business card with an email address and phone number. "My personal cell is on the back."

"Hold on," Carly said. "I'll give you hers."

He held up a hand. "No," he said. "I didn't come over to get her info. I'm sure she controls that information pretty carefully, and she should."

"Please come in, really. She just went to get her nails done. I expect her any time."

Roger smiled. "I'm sure your mother and I will bump into one another again soon."

Yeah, Carly thought. There needs to be more bumping.

7

ALLISON WAS NOT in the mood.

"You knew you had this presentation coming up and you fooled around and fooled around and didn't get ready for it. It's when? – Friday? – and I have grades to get in that have to get done tonight and tomorrow and I don't have time to help you with it." In fact, the grades wouldn't take long. She wanted Carly to be responsible and work to understand the subject herself.

"But I don't get seasons!" Carly said.

"Well, what makes you think I get them?" Allison wasn't sure she did. Something to do with . . . the sun . . . and the earth.

"Mom, you're smart!"

"You're smart, too! Look on the internet! Figure it out."

"I did! I looked a million different places! I still don't get it!"

It's possible she's not just being lazy, Allison thought. Carly had shown signs of Allison's own uncertain spatial reasoning.

"Did you call your father?"

"Mom!" She made it three syllables. "Remember when he tried to help me with fruit fly genes?"

Allison remembered. That attempt had veered into eggs and sperm before Allison had called a halt.

"What are you doing?" Carly said.

Allison was holding a small card and punching a number into her phone with her thumb.

"Roger, Allison Sanders. We're fine, how about you? That's great. Listen, I'm *really* sorry to bother you. No, we don't need anything moved or anything like that. No, nothing to fix."

Carly could not contain her excitement. Allison gestured for her to stop bouncing up and down.

"Why I'm calling is: Do you know anything about seasons? Yes, the four seasons. No, not Vivaldi," she giggled, "not Frankie Valli either. Or the hotel. Right, summer-fall-winter-spring, do you know what causes them? Wait, don't explain now. Carly has to give a presentation about it and she's having some trouble. Could you – oh, that would be so great, really super nice of you."

Carly mouthed *not now! I need an hour!*

Allison considered that her own makeup and attire could use a bit of attention as well.

"Don't rush over. We're just finishing up dinner." Carly mouthed *you are such a liar* and rolled her eyes. "Can you come over in maybe a half-hour? Make it forty-five minutes, okay? That'd be great." Allison listened. "I don't know, let me ask Carly. Do we have a globe?"

Carly shook her head mouthing *I don't think so*. "HI, MR. HOUSMAN," she said.

"Carly says hi," Allison said. "Yes, I'm sure the whole neighborhood heard it. Sorry, looks like no globe. OK, we'll see you, say, quarter to seven? You're so sweet! Thanks, bye."

"Mom," Carly said, "you called him sweet!"

Allison was perfectly aware she had called him sweet. Baby steps.

8

THE DOORBELL RANG at a quarter to seven.

Allison wore a drapey white V-neck blouse with an embroidered Native American design French-tucked into tight black jeans. Kheloni heeled sandals. She had applied a Charlotte Tilbury lipstick that was not-too-*do-me*-red but which she noted with amusement was named Lost Cherry.

Carly had selected some artfully torn jeans and a Ruth Bader Ginsburg T-shirt. Allison had vetoed the heels Carly had wanted to wear, but had allowed her a pair of low platform wedges she had scrounged out of the depths of Allison's closet. Allison hadn't been able to supervise the blush and lipstick and a bit of drama around the eyes, but she had to admit Carly hadn't tarted herself up too much.

The two women being thus prepared to receive astronomical instruction, Allison allowed Carly to open the door to greet Roger Housman.

He was wearing his usual combination of shirt and jeans and boots, altered only by some markers in his shirt pocket. He carried a large pad of graph paper, a ruler, a flashlight, and a globe.

"Well," he said. "I see I am underdressed for this tutoring session."

"You look great!" Carly said. "Come on in!" Allison wilted a little at this reaction more suited to a party than a science lesson.

Allison muted her greeting to smooth out their welcome. "Hello, Roger. Thank you for coming."

He looked around. "Your house is lovely. I could have used some decorating tips on my layout over there. Don't worry about all this hardware," he said. "We'll just need to draw some pictures and think about outer space."

"Don't mind me," Allison said. "I'm just going to get some work done on my laptop here at the breakfast bar. You can spread out in the dining room."

"That'll be fine," Roger said. "First, Carly, tell me how you think seasons work. I don't care how wrong you are, even if you are wrong. Just give it your best shot."

"I was telling Mom that if I had to give my report on Friday I was going to say that a monster space turtle ate a big piece out of the sun in the winter and puked it back up in the springtime."

"Carly!" Allison said. "I heard that."

"I thought you were doing grades," Carly said.

"You would have made an excellent scientist in prehistoric Vietnam," Roger said. "They thought eclipses were caused by a giant frog eating the sun. Try again."

"I don't know," Carly said. "I thought maybe it was because the earth was farther away from the sun in the winter because the earth's orbit isn't a circle."

"A lot of people think that, and you get extra credit for knowing the earth's orbit isn't perfectly circular and it tells me you're going to get this just fine. But no, that's not the reason. Okay, first thing we need to understand is how the sun heats up the surface of the earth in different places and once you have that down, the rest of this is a snap. I need a pan or plate with a nice clean edge about this big so I can draw the earth." He held his hands about ten inches apart.

Carly brought him a small frying pan. He placed it upside down on the graph paper and drew a semicircle with the curve facing the right side of the page. He used the ruler to draw a vertical line between the two ends of the semicircle, then a horizontal line to divide the semicircle in half.

"This is half the earth," he said. The up-and-down line here is the pole – north pole, south pole, see? – and the line cutting it in half is the equator. You know all about these things, right?"

"Oh, yeah," Carly said.

"And the sun is way, way, way off to the right, so far off that we don't have room for it in this drawing. I mean, way off. Way past my house, even. But it's there, and it's hot, and it's huge, and it's sending out rays of sunlight – solar radiation – across space to the earth."

"Okay."

"Do you know why we're starting out by drawing only half the earth to learn about how sunlight heats the earth?"

Carly thought. "Because the sun only can shine on half the earth? At a time?"

"Ms. Sanders," Roger called out, "your daughter has tricked us, she's a genius, I won't need to teach her a thing."

"She tells me that every day," Allison called back.

"You are one hundred percent correct, Carly," Roger said. "So how does the whole earth get warmed by the sun?"

Emboldened by her correct guess, she said, "Because the earth turns around."

"This lesson is going to be short," Roger said. "Right again. So what we learn about the little pieces of earth we can see in this drawing will really apply to the whole earth because . . . because . . . "

"It spins," Carly said.

"Yes!" Roger said. "It rotates. Now, I want you to think of all of these horizontal lines on the graph paper as rays of sunlight coming from the sun. Can you picture that in your mind?"

"Sure."

Allison couldn't catch every word, but she could hear him having Carly repeat what they had just been through. She thought *he's really good with her. He asks her easy but not obvious questions, praises her when she gets things right, responds gently and with humor when she's wrong. He speaks softly.*

She listened as Roger showed Carly how the sun's radiation – the horizontal lines on his graph paper – was concentrated at the equator in the picture he had drawn, but because the solar rays were coming in parallel lines, the further north or south you went, the more the same amount of sunlight got spread over a larger area as the earth's surface sloped away from the equator, so those areas weren't as hot as the equator where the rays were more concentrated. But he didn't just tell her – he had her tell him, asking her questions about the picture he had drawn.

He's leading her right to it. He's hardly had to tell her anything.

"Carly, I'm telling you, we haven't quite gotten to what causes the seasons yet, but if you understand what we just did, actually, what you just did, then you are going to understand the seasons in no time at all. I want you to take a minute and go over what we've just learned in your mind, make sure you've got it down. Just go over it in your head and picture those solar rays all coming in from the sun and hitting the curved surface of the earth. I'm going to take a short break and go say hi to your mom and then I'm going to come back and you are going to explain why different parts of the earth are warmer and cooler in your own words."

"Oh, man, it's a pop quiz."

"Yeah, but there's no grades so you can't fail."

Well, this is encouraging. He's coming over here to do a little mid-season flirting.

He walked into the kitchen and leaned against the breakfast bar. He spoke softly so Carly could not hear.

"Hi," he said.

"Hi," Allison said. "Thanks so much for coming over. Sounds like you're making progress."

"What we're covering isn't terribly tough, but did you hear? She soaked the teaching right up. She's great, super quick. Girls – I wish we could get more of them taking the AP math and science courses in high school and then going into those fields in college. I don't know why young women shy away from tech – it's holding them back in the professions and some great jobs. Hey, do you think your principal would let me bring some female Ph.D. candidates and professors in science and tech to the middle school to talk about the opportunities in STEM?"

He's not flirting. He's concerned, he's inspired.

He's focused on her and on opportunities for girls.

He's looking at me but he's thinking about his idea.

That's okay.

He's real.

Allison said, "I don't see why not."

"Let's talk about that sometime. I want to get back before she gets bored."

"I wouldn't worry about that," Allison said. "She's hoping we're flirting over here. The longer we talk, the better she likes it." *What did I just say? I can't believe I said what I just said.*

He smiled and raised one eyebrow just the tiniest bit.

*Damn. He **was** flirting.*

By being good.

He sat down with Carly again and she went through the reason the sun heats the earth differently at the different distances from the equator in his drawing. She got it right, but he interrupted a couple of times to prompt her to use the technical terms: solar radiation, latitude, rotation.

"Super job," he said. "You got this nailed. Next stop: seasons. Now the thing about this picture is that the sun is shining right down on the equator. Is that what happens all year round?"

"I don't know. I guess so. It's always hot there."

"I want you to pretend that we're traveling through the solar system and we're watching the earth. Now, as you said, the earth rotates, and sure enough, we can see it spinning away here." He slapped at the globe and set it spinning. "But over the course of a year, what else is the earth doing?"

"It's going around the sun."

"Right again, the earth revolves around the sun, and in a year it makes one revolution. Let's look at what happens during that revolution to make the seasons."

He took her into the family room and scooted the central coffee table out of the way. He had her stand in the center of the room. He adjusted the flashlight to make the beam narrow and bright and turned off a couple of table lamps to darken the room.

"You're the sun. You and Justice Ginsburg. You're sending out radiation to the earth and the other planets. In real life you'd be 93 million miles away from the earth, but we're going to pretend." He held the globe at her eye level. "You've seen lots of globes, right? What do you notice about all of them? Are they straight up and down like the earth we drew on the graph paper?"

"No," Carly said. "They always tilt."

"Yes, they always tilt. Like this one I brought. And that's because the earth isn't straight up and down when it's going around the sun, it's tilting. Just remember the tilt, the tilt, the tilt is the most important thing about seasons. And here's what I want you to remember about this tilting – the earth always tilts the same direction, no matter where it is in its orbit around the sun. So now I will be the earth and I'll carry this globe along like it's revolving around you, the sun, tilting all the way."

This is so cool.

Is he doing this to put on a show for me or because it's a good way to show a thirteen-year-old about seasons?

Shame on me. I called him.

Well, so what if he is showing off for me?

I dressed for his visit. Navajo embroidery around the bust – didn't he curate Indian stuff in Lima? – some Lost Cherry on the lips.

Good guys don't just show up in your life three doors down.

If they exist they gotta show up somewhere, though.

Like meteorites gotta land somewhere.

Allison felt herself flush. She took a deep breath. In the family room, Roger the Earth carried the globe around Carly the Sun while she shined the flashlight beam on the globe. Each quarter-turn he asked Carly to identify where the beam was centered on the globe.

This is amazing.

Fun with seasons.

He is completely focused on her.

He repeats things so she'll remember, keeps up the patter so she'll stay focused.

This is a performance.

But not for me.

Maybe for me a little bit?

So clear. Made a little solar system in the family room. It's like he understands how people don't understand.

When they had pantomimed an entire year of the earth's revolution, and Carly had correctly identified where the flashlight beam was centered on different parts of the globe at the different points in the orbit, Roger said:

"You are the smartest sun in the history of suns. Now, I'm going to walk around you a few times very slowly with this globe, and I want you to turn with me and think about your solar rays shining on the earth. Keep the beam on the center of the globe, where your rays will be the most concentrated. Here I go." He walked around her three times and she turned with him, keeping the flashlight beam level and on the globe's middle. He spun the globe as he moved through the revolutions. "Okay, keep all of that in mind and let's come back to the table. Is this all too much to remember?"

"No. I think I'm starting to get it. What you did looks like the drawings on the internet, except in 3D."

"And I'm always in very high-def," Roger said. Carly giggled.

His pitch is just right.

It's hard to joke with kids not quite adults.

He's got the feel.

It's a feel for people.

No wonder they have him asking for money at the U.

When they sat down, he took the frying pan and made two more semicircles on new pages of the graph paper, one with the north pole tilting toward the sun, the other one with it tilting away, with the equator dividing the hemispheres as before, but now tilted like the poles.

"You're going to finish this lesson yourself," he said. He spread the three drawings before her. "We're talking about seasons. We know that four seasons happen during the year, and they blend into each other. Now I just want you to think about the northern hemisphere, and I want you to remember where that beam of solar rays from the flashlight hit the globe as I was revolving around you, and answer this question: Which one of these drawings shows what the earth looks like in the summer?"

She pointed to the drawing with the pole pointed towards the sun.

"*Yes*," Roger said, triumphantly. "Why?"

"Because . . . the sun rays are coming down directly on it."

"On what?"

"On the north part."

"On the . . . ."

"Northern hemisphere."

"Who lives there?"

"We do!" Carly said.

"Yup, we sure do, right about halfway up to the North Pole, right? Do you see that? Here's Ohio. See that?"

"Totally," Carly said.

"What's going on in the southern hemisphere? Look at our rays coming in from the right and remember what we learned before the break."

"The rays are more spread out."

"Because . . . ."

"It's even further away and the sun rays are spread out even more."

"So in the southern hemisphere it's . . . ."

"Winter."

"Ding ding ding! You win a prize."

"What do I win?"

"I'll tell you after we go through the other seasons. Which of these drawings shows winter in the northern hemisphere?"

"This one." She pointed to the picture with the pole pointing away from the sun.

"Reason?"

"The sun rays are all spread out except in the south – southern hemisphere where they are more direct. So it's summer down there."

"Great. Perfect, in fact. Now, remember when I had the globe halfway between summer and winter and I asked you whether the pole pointed toward or away from the sun and you said –"

"Neither one." She pointed to their original drawing. "And the beam was on the equator. So this would be spring or fall, right? Depending on whether it was between winter and summer, or summer and winter." She giggled. "You know what I mean."

"Yes, I do know what you mean, and Miss Carly Sanders, you now know everything that any Ph.D. in astronomy would know about the reasons for the seasons."

"Wow," Carly said.

I've never seen that girl so engaged with anything that didn't relate to clothes, boys, music, or her friends.

Or my love life.

He's hardly looked at me. This top . . . . Would he notice if I changed into something more, more . . . toppy? Probably. And the girl would rat me out.

Carly is absolutely transfixed at being treated with respect and encouragement and humor.

Doubt it hurts the lesson that he's good-looking.

Not hurting me, either.

If he's a manipulator he's the best I've ever seen.

Why am I even thinking that? I'm a jerk.

But I'm a beautiful, smart jerk and I'm a good mom.

And a woman.

And I . . . I'm . . . .

"Okay, Carly, you've done absolutely great. Absolutely great. But you have to do a presentation, right? We've been through a lot of information. Do you think you could describe this back to me in your own words? Could you draw the kind of pictures necessary to show what we've been talking about? It's also on the internet, you know, if you need a refresher and you could probably copy some pictures from there."

"I think so," she said.

Allison had come into the dining room. "I snooped," she said, "so now I understand seasons too and I can help you if you need it."

"What's my prize?" Carly asked.

"Oh, Carly," he said. "Oh, Carly. I am giving you the greatest prize of all. I am giving you *the whole world.*" He slid the globe over in front of her. "It's an amazing place! So much to see and hear and touch and understand! And today you are understanding a huge thing, a whole year's worth of seasons! The world is totally exciting and even though I don't like the word *awesome*, it really is! We should be filled with awe and wonder and curiosity – curiosity! – all the time."

He's talking about learning. The lecture she won't let me give anymore. I wonder if she gets it.

"You're giving me this?"

"You said you didn't have one. I don't need it. The countries are a little out of date in Africa and the old Soviet Union, sorry. You can use it for your presentation – if you want to, that is, if it helps you explain the seasons to your class. You can pick out some cute guy to be the sun and order him around, tell him what to do while you revolve with the tilty earth. I've got a million of these little flashlights, you can have it too. Hey, how about that, I'm also giving you the sun!"

"Oh, Roger," Allison said, "you don't have to do this."

"Don't have to. Want to. But here's the thing: I'm going to come back tomorrow evening and you are going to give me your presentation, Carly. Arrange the information in any way that makes sense to you because that's the way it will probably make most sense to your classmates. Maybe make the drawings in a PowerPoint. You know how to do graphics in PowerPoint?"

"Seventh graders can diagram the Death Star in a PowerPoint," Allison said.

He looked up at Allison for a moment before addressing Carly again. "I suggest that you take all this stuff back to your room – that's where you usually do homework and stuff, right? I know you got a computer and a printer up there, right?" Allison nodded. "Go through what we did, get it fixed in your mind, maybe do it alongside the stuff from your textbook and the internet that wasn't clear to you before, and that will also help you totally remember and nail this down in that impressive brain of yours."

Allison said, "I think that is a splendid idea," and gave Carly a look.

"Are you going to stay for a while? I want to stay," Carly said.

He's basically telling her to make herself scarce.

That's an initiative I need to reinforce.

"Room," Allison said. "Presentation. Door closed. Please." Her accompanying look underlined the seriousness of the suggestion. But she winked at her daughter.

"Oh. All right." Carly dragged herself up the stairs to her bedroom at the top of the stairs with a practiced display of ostentatious teengirl dramatics and slowly closed the door behind her, making sure the latch engaged with sufficient definition and volume to be heard at the couch below her.

Roger returned the family room furniture to its pre-solar system configuration. Allison said, "I happen to have a bottle of wine in the fridge that has an extremely colorful label."

"Sure," he said. "That would be nice after hauling the earth around a few revolutions."

She poured their glasses and gestured for him to sit on the couch. She sat a little more towards the middle than before. So did he.

Allison said, "You meant that, didn't you, about being filled with wonder all the time?"

"It's the only way to live. And the more you know about the world, the closer you come to what is awesome, and the more awesome things you find. But I also do hate the word *awesome* these days, which has been degraded as it's now used to describe everything from autotuned adolescent vocalists to very average – well, very average everything."

"George Eliot would never have said that any average thing was awesome," Allison said.

"Well, exactly," Roger said. "Meanings can evolve over time, sure, but *awesome* tells you on its face what it means, something that inspires awe, and any use of it to describe something ordinary is . . . it's . . . ."

Allison said, "Basically, a lie."

Roger faced her and his look turned near-fierce. "*Yes!*" he hissed. "Yes. Misusing words is lazy, sometimes just ignorant, but sometimes fraud. It leads to false thinking and false art, too." His face softened but his eyes remained urgent. "Our favorite authors, the ones we mentioned the other day? Some of them used a lot of words, and we may not always have liked what those words said, but at least they used the words precisely to express their intention, and why we *must* continue to honor them as you do in your classes, hold them up and say *read this and learn.*"

Allison felt her own eyes igniting. "Oh, yes! And *cut the crap,* right? Don't live by slogans and sayings and memes! See the vapid and self-centered for the cartoons they are! Live truly by the evidence of your own senses and the wisdom of those who have studied the world and themselves and humanity with care and respect!"

"And reported it with clarity," Roger said. He picked up a copy of *Slouching Towards Bethlehem* from an end table and waved it.

They were both a little breathless, and more than a little surprised by the turn their conversation had taken. They sipped their wine.

"I think we're going to be good neighbors," Roger said.

"I have a feeling Carly is going to try to find other things to claim to be confused about now."

"She's a peach. Smart, she was ahead of the lesson most of the time. And I was thinking: 'You know, Carly reflects very well on that mother of hers.'"

"Thank you." Allison held out her glass and they clinked. This time, the clink had a meaning that they both understood. "You're very sweet."

Allison tried to think of something else to say that wouldn't be too forward, but forward enough.

They chatted a little about the neighborhood, enough to exhaust and refresh their glasses.

Roger said, "Did she say she was giving her presentation on Friday?"

"She's a last-minute kind of gal," Allison said.

"It's going to go great," he said, "and she's already thinking about what guy she's going to pick out to be the sun. In fact, that may be all she's thinking about right now." *No*, Allison thought, *she's thinking about what we're up to down here*. "I need to remind her to turn off the room lights and close the blinds if she's going to do the flashlight thing. The class is gonna flip," he said, "and so will her teacher, and they're never going to forget about Ms. Carly Sanders's seasons lesson."

"Neither will I, Roger. Neither will I."

Roger smiled. "I was thinking maybe I could take you and Carly to dinner on Saturday to celebrate the success of her dramatic presentation of the four seasons."

Allison was not expecting this and was more thrilled than she could recall ever having been at the suggestion of a date, or something like one.

Time to keep my head about me.

Sorry, Carly.

Not that sorry.

"That is a wonderful, generous idea, but Carly's almost fourteen. She and I don't have to be a package deal all the time."

"Well," he said, "okay, but –"

"Believe me," Allison said, "she won't like it, but she'll get it. And then she'll think about it and her imagination will go into overdrive and then she'll like it. I'll let her invite a friend over and they can gossip about us."

They talked a little more as they finished the bottle.

Roger stood.

"I'll come back tomorrow to see if she still gets it," he said. "The lesson, I mean."

"Thank you again," Allison said, rising and standing a little closer now. "You were amazing. I was actually moved by how you unpacked it all for her and let her put it all back together on her own. That's a gift."

"I'll see you tomorrow and look forward to Saturday."

Allison said, "I didn't win Miss Ohio, but I'll tell you why the winner won."

"And I'll tell you the real reason we have seasons," Roger said, and did that thing with his eyebrow again.

"You're not exactly the boy next door, are you?" she said.

"Three doors down," he said. "The one your mom warned you about."

"The one I ignored my mom's warnings about," she said.

"I came with my arms full," he said. "They seem to be empty now."

"I always hoped to know a man who could move the earth," she said.

They both chuckled a little uneasily.

She moved into him. He took her hands in his.

Allison glanced to the top of the stairs and saw the sliver of light she expected to see.

They kissed sweetly and briefly, and sweetly, briefly, again.

"Good night," Allison said.

"Dress rehearsal tomorrow," he said. "Same time, here, if that works for you."

Allison closed the door behind him. From the top of the stairs, *woo hoo!*

The Pledge and the Pi

1

IT HAD NEVER occurred to Dolly Ramos that she would ever tire of sorority life. But she had recently felt a sameness in the late-night girl talk, the fraternity parties, even the meals prepared by the house's chef. She had wearied of the scramble to rush the most popular young women entering the university, who, she observed, were themselves exhibiting a certain sameness.

Jaded as a junior? She shook off the thought.

She did not dislike Pi Sigma Rho or the women in it. She liked her sisters, a handful of them quite a lot. There were some obvious benefits to sorority life, although the women in the dorms seemed to have enhanced access to the general run of men at the U and, if not more fun than a barrel of monkeys, at least fun equivalent to a barrel of monkeys, while she seemed to be having maybe a bushel-of-monkeys amount of fun. But the sorority house had bigger closets than the dorms and the bathrooms weren't as drafty. That wasn't nothing.

Tonight, another mixer with Iota Tau Omicron, Pi Sigma's brother fraternity at the U.

The mixers were okay. You didn't have to drive to them, so you could drink. The local law usually looked the other way unless there was trouble.

She wasn't sure about the quality of men in the fraternities compared to those to be found in the general campus population. Maybe a little more sophisticated, although the passed-out bodies in the frat-house common room in the small hours of Sunday mornings, which, thankfully, she had only had to tiptoe around a couple of times, looked like they might have been staged by Tarantino. Drinking-until-comatose aside, there might have been a little more money behind these guys than the dorm guys. And, almost certainly, a little more ambition, even if some of it seemed to have been gifted from a mom and dad looking to pass along a family business. Among them, surely there was a man of character and class; wouldn't hurt if he had a dollar or three. So she was happy enough to have pledged Pi Sigma Rho and to have at least slightly enhanced access to the at least lightly-curated fraternity men.

Still, she felt an itch that Greek life just wasn't scratching.

She looked around the room at the men and women not long out of high school. We're all playing at being adults, she thought, trying this being-away-from-home thing on for size, except that, catastrophe aside, there was no going back to mom and dad. She was twenty-one, almost twenty-two. She wasn't sure what she wanted to do, except that she was pretty sure she wanted to get away from the university town that existed pretty much only as a place name for the U's campus. She was ready as well to move from the endless plains that surrounded the town, and even the nearby mountains. The land was beautiful, she acknowledged. But it didn't pay money, and it didn't produce single men of appropriate age and means in commercial retail quantities, and, unless you let yourself get sucked in to the feckless UFO or Bigfoot crowds that seemed drawn to the area, it was not a source of adventure, at least of the kind that she imagined would give her life meaning.

Tonight, she did not expect to find meaning for her life among the fraternity guys.

But, you never know.

Take that sore thumb over there.

Well, maybe not so sore.

Maybe not a thumb, either.

Tall; more, big. Standing alone, holding a red Solo cup. Powerfully built under his slacks and jacket. The only guy in the place wearing a jacket. It was a really nice jacket; getting something cut to his size, in what looked like a light merino weave, that would have been a project and not cheap. But it made him seem of another time and place. No matter how nice he looked, guys just didn't wear jackets anymore, and the creased slacks should have been jeans if he wanted to fit in. Blond, short brush cut. A little weatherbeaten but a strong, square face whose even features bespoke intelligence and even a kind of lived-in manliness, even for a guy who probably wasn't yet twenty. But those features needed to be smiling. He was trying to look glad to be there, but the broad Scandinavian brushstrokes on his handsome head were strained.

Dolly approached him and said, "I don't think I've seen you at one of these before."

"I'm just a pledge," he said. "They let us come to this one, probably to show us all the pretty sisters."

"Probably, and I'll thank you for the compliment," she said. "What's your name?"

"Vernon Compton."

"I'm Dolly," she said. She noted his eyes widening slightly at this information, but she was used to some reaction when she introduced herself with this uncommon name. She held out her hand and Vernon shook it. She appreciated the gentleness with which he took her small hand in his large one, but she showed him her ranch-girl grip. "Short for Dahlia. My mother's favorite flower. I know it's kind of a funny name, but I've gotten used –"

"Oh, no," Vernon said, looking at her directly for the first time as his features softened. "Dolly is a very beautiful name."

"Oh . . . thank you." Dolly didn't get that reaction very often. "Last name Ramos."

"May I call you Dolly?" Vernon asked.

No one had ever asked permission to call her the name everyone called her. "Yeah, sure, it's like almost my only name. No one calls me Dahlia unless I'm being naughty."

"Dolly," he said, nodding, trying out the sound of it. "I'm sure you're never naughty. It's almost impossible to be naughty these days, seems like you can do anything. No one's supposed to be ashamed of anything."

"You sound like you don't entirely approve of that state of affairs," she said.

He shrugged. "Gotta go with it," he said. "Times change."

This guy was – what, Dolly thought, eighteen, nineteen? Like he'd lived through times when there was a lot of shaming going on?

"I wanted to tell you I really like what you have on," she said.

"Thank you, miss" – caught himself – "Dolly. It's not right," he said. "I showed up on campus with the wrong stuff. And maybe a little warm for this tonight. I need to go shopping."

"I'll go with you," Dolly said.

"Oh," Vernon said. "Wow. That is super nice of you. Be honest with you, I didn't think sorority actives were even allowed to talk to pledges, much less be out with them. Even though shopping isn't really a date, is it?"

"I won't worry about the rules if you won't," Dolly said. "Or what we call a shopping trip."

Vernon smiled and tried to look her over a bit more carefully. What he saw was a slender brunette; the hair was gleaming but had an ignored look about it, straight down to her shoulders but a big lock also swooped down almost to her eyes. Those eyes were brown and accompanied smooth tan-toned skin that probably came from Ramos, whoever he or she was. Strong, lean features; an open, honest look, but feminine. Square shouldered, good posture – posture, very important – but it was the arms and legs emerging from the sleeveless top and short skirt that got his attention. They were muscular, no fat on them, maybe even just a little ropy. Good, sturdy limbs. Topped off by eyes that one could call mischievous, but what might have been mischief in others ran deeper with her; maybe a little danger peeking out from behind those peeps.

Vernon tried to take it all in without being too obvious. He failed in that, but spoke for the first time with a little more confidence. "Yeah," he said, "I don't much care for rules, either, unless I'm making them."

"That's what I think, too," Dolly said. She was starting to like this big guy. Young, but put together nicely. A little bashful, but there was a finish to him, like he was raised right.

"I sounded a little arrogant there," he said. "Truth is, I don't like to make rules, either. Are you sure it's okay for an upperclass active to talk to me?"

She ignored the question. "Don't take this the wrong way," Dolly said, "but you don't exactly seem like the pledge type, not for Iota Tau anyway."

"I'm not," he said. "I'm the first person from my family to go to college. My Pop wanted me to pledge. His downtown buddies told him this was the one to pledge, so here I am."

"What are you thinking about it?"

"The guys are okay," he said. "The house will probably be better than the dorm, although I'm liking the dorm just fine so far. I'll tell you, though, I could do without the process."

"Rush is definitely a pain," Dolly said, "even for sororities. Although thank God we've never had a fatality here or even any major hospitalizations. There's an arrest from time to time, but pretty much minor stuff. The U and the national Greek councils have really been cracking down on the worst of it."

"It can still be pretty bad," Vernon said.

"What have they got you doing?" she said. "Or is it a big secret?"

"Some of the rituals are absolutely secret. The hazing

stuff is supposed to be secret, too, although . . . ," his eyes narrowed and his smile turned from pasted-on to conspiratorial as he regarded this attractive woman with a wild girlish streak behind her eyes, "although, I might tell you."

2

THE RUSH CO-CHAIRS Doyle Lindstrom and Bucky Jaynes had come to Vernon with what they said was his last task before the committee decided on his candidacy for Iota Tau. They seemed nervous.

"We're not saying you can't get in if you won't do this," Doyle said, "but if you pull this off, you're not only a lock, you're an instant legend at Iota Tau and the U, and I mean forever. Although you may have to be a secret legend for reasons you'll understand in a minute. Just listen, then we'll try to answer questions, but some of this you'll have to improvise."

Doyle took a deep breath and started in. "U is playing Masterson College here this weekend. Masterson is about a hundred-fifty miles west of here."

"I know it," Vernon said. Did they think he hadn't lived on these plains his entire life?

Doyle went on. "They used to be the Masterson Paiutes, but they got tired of all the fuss about the Indian name so they renamed themselves the Masterson Mastiffs, the Mighty Mastiffs, I think. Everybody loves a dog, right? And dogs don't complain about being exploited. So they've got this mastiff as their mascot now. Too bad, that Paiute mascot was badass, especially the years when it was a chick."

"Is this about stealing a mascot?" Vernon said. "Man,

me and my buddies were the James Gang of mascot thieves in high school. So far, I'm in."

Doyle and Bucky looked at each other. Doyle said, "You never stole a mascot like this one. Let me finish. This isn't some halfassed statue of a dog. This is a real live mastiff. Big dog, you know? Real big. They got an alum over there that breeds these gigantic Italian mastiffs."

"Cane corsos," Bucky said. "It's pronounced 'connie corso.' I studied up on 'em."

"Okay, whatever," Doyle said. "Anyway, this alum donates the use of a dog to the college to trot out on game days. But he gets to pick out the dog. The college doesn't get to pick out some dog that's bred for gentleness and niceness, maybe an older female, even. No. The alum sends them this intact breeding male he calls 'Master' – get it? – that's all skittish and aggressive and mean as hell – I mean, certifiably vicious – and this thing weighs close to a hundred pounds. I gotta say, the dog is gorgeous. All black, incredible-looking animal.

"But this dog – he's a huge risk. I can't believe they have him out on the sidelines. We've heard he's hurt people, at least one big lawsuit, and they don't let him around kids. The word around Masterson is that the alum had to grease some palms to keep the county from putting the beast down. He's got two handlers, big guys, each with a leash and a separate collar on the dog in case one fails or one of the guys somehow lets go.

"So you can imagine, game day rolls around, and he's all hepped up when they get him out of his crate and take him out to the field, and when the crowd starts screaming and the bands are playing and the teams run out, he goes absolutely nuts, barking and pulling on those leashes like he wants to attack the opponent. Although he'd be just as likely to attack the Masterson players and take out a couple of rows of fans and the drum majorette while he was at it.

"But the crowd loves this crazy howling slobbering dog, absolutely adores him. They scream when he starts in to bark and carry on, and that just gets him more excited. His picture is on all the Masterson stuff. You should see the merch they move every week. What they don't know is that the college is worried enough about this monster that each one of those handlers has a tranq gun under his Mighty Mastiff jacket in case Master threatens to get loose.

"So here's the deal: Lowell Suggs – you know Lowell? – his brother and another buddy from here go to Masterson and they both work for the athletic department. They're practice squad, didn't make the team this year, but the department puts them on the payroll as gofers, so they can hang around the team on game day. They hate this fucking dog. They have to work around him and they're scared of him, and they're big guys themselves. I'll come back to them in a minute, just wanted you to know how I know all this.

"So for away games the alum breeder sends the dog in a trailer the night before with the two big guys. Like a small horse trailer. So the dog isn't traveling on game day. Well, good old Master doesn't like to travel and he doesn't like to be caged. But it turns out he's kind of like those birds that calm down when you put a black cloth over their cage, you know? As long as he's all in the dark, he's more docile, not constantly launching himself like he would at the bars of a regular cage. They actually nail the SOB into a wooden crate. Hey, come to think of it, he really is a son of a bitch, isn't he? Heh. He fits in it, but they don't give him lots of room to bang around where he might hurt himself, so it's not a huge crate. It's all padded, too. It's not airtight so he can breathe, and they plan the travel to minimize the time he's in the crate. And, of course, when they finally open it up, he's batshit and ready for his batshit act for the crowd."

Vernon knew where this was going. He didn't like it. But he felt obliged to listen with respect to his possible future brothers and this sketchy rush assignment.

"Now, Lowell's brother and his buddy, they have access to this trailer. The two handlers from the alum breeder drive the rig to a motel so they can get some sleep and some breakfast before they come back and get Master leashed up for the game. Our guys meet them at the motel when they arrive and get the keys so they can drive the truck to the secure gated parking area for the away team. The keys include the keys to the trailer."

Doyle stopped talking and reached for his wallet. "This is the key card to open the gate to the parking."

"Let's see," Vernon said. "You haven't actually said it out loud, but the plan is to snatch the dog." Doyle and Bucky nodded slightly. "What laws would I be breaking? I'd have university access to the lot with your card there. The trailer would be open, courtesy Suggs brother and buddy. Would going into the trailer be burglary? Don't know, maybe. Probably. Taking the dog in the crate would be stealing, but it would be mascot-stealing. My Pop, he's kind of a boys-will-be-boys guy."

The laws, Vernon thought, not so much. Local politicians have frats in their cross-hairs. Masterson may have been two-plus hours away by car, but it was in the same county as Vernon's ass listening to this scheme, and located at the county seat to boot, where it contributed district attorneys and judges to the distinguished law enforcement infrastructure that was called upon to evaluate the legality of the public activities of the scholars attending the U.

"Man, I don't know. I lived the life of the blessed when I was a teenager. Hell, I still am a teenager. But not a single arrest or problem, not for drinking, not for the mascot stuff, nothing. I'm clean. I cannot get caught with that dog, no matter that it's a prank. Cannot. So what's the risk of getting caught here? Are there cameras? Guards?"

They assured them there were none.

"This is a live animal. It can't live without food or water," Vernon said.

"Jesus, forgot to tell you. They've got a big plastic jug stuck on the inside of the crate and the dog can get some water out of a little spigot thing that he activates by nudging on it. And as soon as the game starts and Masterson has freaked out over the missing Master, someone will tell them where to find the dog. It won't starve and as long as it stays in its crate it may not be happy but it won't know what's going on or give much of a shit. Where you stash it, that's your problem. One more thing."

"Only one?" Vernon said.

"This thing is heavy," Doyle said, "and it's in a wood crate. I'll bet it weighs 125 at least. And the dog will probably bang around in the crate and bark like crazy, at least at first. Tough to deal with. Do not, repeat, do not open that crate to look at the dog, even for a peek. The thing is nailed shut for a reason and the two guys from the breeder are professional dog handlers."

"Weight's not a problem," Vernon said. He'd lifted that and more for hours at a time. "I can lift and manipulate it and I'll have a dolly if I need one. My Jeep should hold a crate if it's not too big. Need to give some thought to where to take the thing so it's safe and they can find it easily without finding me." Vernon knew the countryside around the town and thought there were several places he could safely leave the crate.

He had a thought. "What about Lowell's brother and his buddy? They'll be suspected immediately."

"Number one, they hate the dog. Number two, they hate being at Masterson."

"Fine," Vernon said. "Do they hate not being in jail?"

"Number three," Doyle said, "after you leave, they're going to lock the trailer back up and then pick the lock with burglar tools, which will make marks, they'll make sure of that. Even if they don't get it open using the tools, it'll look like that's how it was done, and the thief just locked it back up."

"Christ," Vernon said, "this is getting more illegal by the minute." Also, pretty ingenious.

"I asked you if you knew Lowell Suggs," Doyle said. "His brother is even more Suggsish."

Swiping a mascot; classic prank. Who had ever gone to jail for that? Who had ever even ended up with anything other than a misdemeanor or a slap on the wrist? Only the possible harm to the live animal really bothered him, even if it was a monster with murder in its eye.

"What do you think?" Doyle said. "Like I said, no shame in declining."

"Who knows about this?" Vernon said.

"Me, Bucky, and Lowell, and Dick Dunham got us this pass, but he doesn't know much other than there's a prank involved. And one guy other than Bucky and me on the rush committee. And Lowell's brother and his buddy."

Vernon could not believe it. He knew if he did it, he'd go down. Too many people knew. Too many moving parts. "The Cosa Nostras tattle on each other, and they've taken a blood oath not to," he said.

"We all want to be legends, too," Bucky said.

Vernon said he'd sleep on it and give them an answer the next day.

He slept on it. Considered all the angles, at least the angles he could think of. Thought about what made sense, and what did not. Slept well that night.

Late the next afternoon he went looking for Doyle Lindstrom.

3

DOLLY THREW HER head back and emitted a long, loud, rather unladylike laugh. "You have got to be kidding!" she said.

"Shhhh," Vernon said.

They had moved outside to the wraparound veranda on the side of the frat house.

"Good lord, that's the stupidest thing I ever heard," she said. "It's not that it can't work, it's that even if it does the cops will figure it out in about ten minutes. You could have a record, even go to jail."

"Mm," Vernon said.

"What did you tell them?" Dolly said.

Vernon reached into his wallet and pulled out the gate

key for the visitors parking. He raised it to eye level and gave it a shake.

Dolly Ramos's heart began to race. "Wait a minute," she said. "Why are you telling *me*?"

"I told you," he said. "Dolly is a beautiful name."

She searched his eyes, his face, for a clue to his meaning. His trunk began to shake; he was chuckling, a near-silent *hee-hee-hee*. His eyes were merry, full of life.

"Trust me," he said.

What was it about this large young man, not much more than a boy, really, of so few words? And most of the words were kind, and sensible, and respectful. They'd been talking for almost an hour, and he hadn't really even hit on her. He was even shy about maybe going shopping with her.

"I think maybe I do," she said.

He cocked an eyebrow at her.

"Let's go," she said.

4

THEY AGREED TO separate and speak with other people at the mixer for a while, then sneak out to change and get some rest. He picked her up a couple of blocks from the Pi Sigma house at 2:15 Saturday morning. On mixer nights and on nights before football weekends, the house mother wasn't too strict about comings and goings.

"I feel like Bonnie Parker," she said.

"You're prettier than Faye Dunaway," he said.

She laughed. "I thought you said I could trust you."

"I didn't say you *could* trust me," he said. "I just said 'trust me.' And anyway, you are prettier than her."

"Well," she said, "I can't say that you're prettier than Warren Beatty. But 'pretty' men – eh. And you're much, much bigger. And way prettier than Clyde Barrow. And probably more trustworthy than either of them."

"Clyde was a small man but he was absolute hell with firearms and cars," Vernon said.

"Well," Dolly said, "here's hoping we won't need any particular skill with either."

"For sure," Vernon said. "But just in case, there's a .38 in the glove compartment. And a nine under my seat."

Dolly opened the glove compartment and saw the revolver. She closed it right up and turned to Vernon. She had been a little nervous. Now she was concerned. She considered that she did not really know this guy that well.

"All legal," he said. "If Master plays his part in this, we should be just fine."

"You seem oddly calm about all this," she said.

"Yeah," he said. "I think we're going to come out of this okay."

"Do you really? What do you mean, 'if Master plays his part'?"

"Trust and be cool," he said. "Didn't Reagan say that? Something like that. This is the start of your legend. If Pi Sigma ever expands its house, they'll call it the Dolly Ramos wing."

She did not know what he meant by that, but there was something in his voice that reassured her. She knew she was about to do something crazy but she had a vision of him wrapping her in those giant arms and holding off all harms.

They approached the visitors parking area. The key card worked and they drove in.

"There's the pickup with the trailer," Vernon said. "Right where they said, away from the lights a little. Good job so far. I'm going to drive by a couple of times to see if we scare up any witnesses or security. Help me look, but if I decide the time is right and I stop, get down. Suggs's brother and his buddy are watching for us somewhere, but they're probably out of sight."

"Wait," she said. "Aren't you going to need help with that crate? I thought that's why I came along."

"No," he said. "I can lift it and since that dog's going to start making noise right away, I need to move it into the back as fast as I can so we can close up and move out. You just stay down when I stop."

Vernon drove slowly through the lot. There were just a few cars there and the pickup with the trailer.

"Okay, get down *now*," Vernon said. He had rolled to a stop with the back of the SUV just a few feet from the back of the trailer. He popped the rear hatch from inside the SUV, hopped out, closed the door just far enough to shut the interior light off, and ran to the back of the trailer.

The doors opened right up. The crate was there in the middle of the floor. It began to rock as soon as Vernon put one foot into the trailer to reach and drag it toward him. The rocking was accompanied by muffled barking and growling. Vernon paused for a moment to listen to it. Then he grabbed the crate by two corners and lifted it cleanly out of the trailer and into the back of the SUV. He closed the SUV hatch by hand then quietly closed the trailer doors. He threw his big body back behind the wheel and closed the car door as quietly as he could. Then he drove slowly out of the lot. In the rearview mirror he could see two figures in the distance. One of them waved.

"You moved that crate like it was nothing," she said.

"It is nothing," he said.

"It looked heavy."

"I've done a fair bit of farm work," he said. "Requires some lifting."

Dolly looked out at the quiet streets. Just a few students walking around, probably drunk on a game's-eve night.

"If you didn't need help, why did I come along?" she said.

Vernon smiled as his eyes darted left and right for signs of detection or pursuit, then turned to her and said: "I believe you know the answer to that question."

Dolly didn't know, or didn't think she knew, but then she thought maybe she did know.

"Because I'm crazy?"

"No ma'am. Furthest thing from."

"Because you are?"

"Maybe, but that's not the reason."

The SUV's big engine burbled and hummed as they cruised leisurely back to the main drag.

"Because this whole thing's crazy," she said.

"And . . . "

"And I need more crazy in my life, and so do you, and this whole crazy thing is it."

Vernon smiled out the windshield. "So smart," he said. "I knew I was right about you. I could feel it, see it in the sparkle of your eye. Dolly. Damn. Dolly. I'm honored to have you alongside. Top-shelf crazy is hard come by. When it's dropped in your lap it should be shared with those who need and appreciate it."

This big country boy is a philosopher of crazy, but cool.

"I have a real good feeling that tonight is going to be crazy in ways you don't quite expect. But I'll repay your trust, Miss Dolly, I will."

She couldn't put her finger on why his words worked to settle her.

There were only a few lights on the main streets they took out of town. The crate rocked and barked from time to time. Before long they were headed southwest on State Route 47 across the plains.

"Where are we going?" Dolly said. "And why are you driving so slowly?"

"You only think I'm driving slow because no one drives the speed limit on these state highways," Vernon said. "I'm right at the limit now. And I'm still thinking about what we're going to do with old Master here. Got a pretty good notion, though. How you doing back there, boy?"

More rocking and barking.

"How are you doing, Dolly?" he said.

"I've never had a first date quite like this," she said.

"'First date,'" he said. "I like the sound of that."

"Me too," she said, and she reached out and squeezed his arm with both hands.

"I'm not the hottest tamale in the combo plate," Vernon said, "but I know how to show a girl a good time. Although never one quite like you. Guess you're a woman, aren't you? Well, I'm having a good time so far. And unless I miss my guess, the time is about to get even better."

"What makes you say that?" she said.

"Look in the rearview on your side," he said.

"My God, it's cops!" she said. The flashing lights were way behind them, but there was no one else on the road. The authorities were after them. "What's happened? Where did they come from?"

"Listen to me," Vernon said. "I want you to assume that whatever happens, you are not going to get in any trouble. You went for a drive with me after the party and just got caught up in this thing. You assume that, okay?" Dolly nodded. "Now, answer this question: Do you want me to stop?"

What in the name of perdition did this country boy think was going to happen? His calm and the small smile he had on his face as he studied the road ahead comforted her.

"In for a dime, in for a dollar," she said.

"I knew it," he said. "You're a sport. I guarantee you'll be the toast of Pi Sigma when this is all over."

She didn't tell him that she already was, for reasons she might tell him later.

The crate had been quiet. It resumed rocking and barking when he gave the SUV a little more gas.

Vernon dropped his voice to just above a whisper. "Do me a favor," he said. "Listen to that barking." He reached back and banged on the crate. "Hey, Master, you lousy mutt!" This inspired more barking and snarling.

"What are you doing?" Dolly said. "Don't provoke him."

"Keep listening," he whispered. Vernon reached back and grabbed the corner of the crate and shook it a little. More barking and snarling and rocking.

"One more," he said. "My sophomore team could whip your Mighty Mastiffs!" he yelled, and he banged his huge fist on the top of the crate. The rocking became even more fierce, accompanied by more barking

She looked at the crate oddly. Then she looked at Vernon oddly.

"Keep what you just heard in mind," he said. "Now I've got this bus up to ninety and we've been cruising along here for several minutes since we saw the lights. You notice anything?"

"Yeah," she said. "They're not catching us and they don't seem to be getting any closer."

"Bingo," he said. "And no heat from the other direction. They haven't called for any help, apparently."

Dolly tried to pull together what Vernon was thinking. There was something out there, just beyond her reach.

"Okay," he said. "It's time to lose these guys for a while." He punched the gas and the SUV roared and accelerated like it had just left the pad at Cape Canaveral.

"What are you doing?" Dolly said. "You can't outrun the cops with their souped-up engines!"

"As you noticed," he said, "they weren't catching us at ninety, and we'll lose them at one-twenty."

"One-twenty!"

"This is a Jeep Grand Cherokee Trackhawk," he said. "It produces over seven hundred horsepower. It laughs at 120 so in the unlikely event those cop lights don't get smaller and smaller, which I expect they will, and soon, I've got a lot more room on this speedometer."

"You are crazy, aren't you?" she said, but there was a hint of admiration in it.

"Yes, ma'am," he said. "I am. But you said you'd trust

me. And as I believe we have discovered, you're a little crazy too."

"I must be," she said. "Just don't get us killed."

"Zero chance of that. I know these roads and this vehicle. Both can handle the speed, but when those lights disappear behind the hills we are starting to put between us, we're going to slow down and make a turn."

A couple of minutes passed. "Okay, we turn here," he said. "Hang on, we have to get out of range so they can't see us when they come to that intersection." The SUV roared its approval of the gulp of gas it seldom saw and leapt ahead even faster than before.

"Holy mother," Dolly said.

"We'll be slowing shortly," Vernon said. "Get ready to take stock."

Dolly could hardly believe the speed at which they were traveling. The minutes ticked by; Vernon seemed to have a destination in mind but wasn't sharing. Meanwhile, Dolly returned to trying to piece together what was happening. The cops couldn't catch them at ninety. Vernon wasn't afraid of getting stopped. And he wanted her to listen to the barking.

"My God," she said, "forget the dog, the speeding alone is going to bust you."

Vernon shook his head. "Two things," he said. "One, except for those police chasing us, every cop in the county is in town busting the drinking that goes on the Friday nights before games."

"What's number two?"

"Number two is: The road we've been on for the last ten

minutes is private. We're on land owned by my family. No speed limit, no cops."

Nice clothes; nice car; nice highway; nice man.

"You don't give a damn about pledging Iota Tau, do you?" Dolly said.

"No," Vernon said.

"You're not a country hick, are you?"

"Oh, yes ma'am, I am," he laughed. "Most definitely."

"I just realized. I'd sort of forgotten your last name. The road we took out of town, we passed the Compton School of Animal Husbandry," she said.

He shook with that silent chuckle of his. "Great-Grampa," he said, "and my Pop."

"You're a rich country hick," she said.

"Not yet," he said.

"Your Pop could buy and sell the pops of every one of those brothers, couldn't he?"

He couldn't stop chuckling. "He has, a couple of 'em."

"And that's why Iota Tau is recruiting this very unfratty guy," Dolly said.

"My guess," he said.

"You got any other guesses?" she said.

He glanced away from the road long enough to flash his toothiest smile of the evening. "Yeah," he said, "do you?"

"This is a set-up."

"Shit!" he shouted, "You are every bit as sharp as I thought you'd be. Oops, sorry about the language."

"Don't worry about the language. I hear much worse around the sorority."

"No," he said. "I was raised not to curse around ladies, and you are that."

So sweet.

"Those assho – those jerks want to embarrass you," Dolly said. "The fix is in, somehow."

"Not exactly a fix," he said. "Remember the first thing you said to me when I told you about this?"

"Yeah, I said it was the stupidest thing I'd ever heard."

"You did say that," he said. He was quiet as he concentrated on the road ahead. "And, of course, you were absolutely right."

"We've never really been at risk, have we?" she said.

"I believe not." Vernon's voice became serious. "I will never, ever put you at risk."

Will, never, ever. Looking ahead. Huh. She thought about remarking on this observation but kept her peace, surprising herself with the thought that it didn't feel all that presumptuous to her.

She moved to a different thought and pulled out her phone.

"I'm not calling anyone," she said.

"I know," he said, and then began to laugh his high-pitched breathy laugh, *hee-hee-hee*, *hee-hee-hee*, sounding so odd coming from that barrel chest. "It took a day-and-a-half for this to dawn on me, and you got it in a half-hour."

She typed in a search and when the images came up, she scrolled through them.

Hee-hee-hee, he laughed, louder now.

Hee-hee-hee.

She looked at the dozens of pictures of Master the Mastiff on game day. Sitting quietly. Looking noble. Slurping a kid's ice cream cone to the amusement of the kid and several other kids. A collar and a slack leash held by one man, who was smiling and posing for pictures himself with his head right next to Master's massive gourd. An absolutely stunning dog.

Hee-hee-hee. "You ever hear a dog with such a limited vocabulary?" Vernon said. "Listen for when we go over this train crossing. Hang on, we're going to go –"

The Jeep lifted off its springs and banged back down. "—a little airborne."

Dolly's eyes got big.

Vernon said, "You ever hear a dog say *ow, goddammit* before? And bark the same bark about every four, five times?"

"SHIT!" she said. "I wasn't raised good like you! So I say SHIT!" She turned around and banged on the crate. "Whoever you are in there, get out!"

"Hold on, Dolly," Vernon said. "Hey," he hollered, "can you open that up from the inside? I brought a crowbar."

They heard what sounded like a *yeah*.

"Just to be safe," he said, "get that .38 out of the glove box."

"I know how to use a pistol," she said.

"I know," he said. "You were raised on a farm, weren't you? Ranch girl."

How in the world did he know that? "I was, 'til I was fifteen," she said, "But how –"

"Don't shoot," the crate yelled. "I'm not armed. Take me a second to unclip this thing. Just hang on."

Vernon slowed and pulled off the road.

"You knew all along," she said.

"I didn't know," he said. "I figured."

"Too stupid, wasn't it?" she said.

"They thought I was too stupid not to believe them," Vernon said. "Country boy. The moment I realized the whole fraternity could be suspended for this, I started thinking."

"But the cops," she said.

He smiled. *Hee-hee-hee*. "We'll deal with the cops later," he said.

The crate started banging and after a few bangs the top opened a crack, then more, and after a few more moments a head appeared.

"Well," Vernon said, "I was wrong about that. I figured it would be a kid."

"Oh," Dolly said, "you're a –"

"You can say it," the man said. "Little person, dwarf, midget, vertically challenged, I don't care. I'm actually half-way making a living out of it. Gotta do something other than Social Security."

"What's your name, man?" Vernon said.

"Lewis," the man said. "Lewis Billups."

"Vernon and Dolly. Where's the player?"

"Still in the box here," Lewis said. He pulled out a digital recorder. "They only gave me six clips of barking and that."

"How much they pay you?" Vernon said.

"Grand," Lewis said.

"Cash money in hand?"

"Half," Lewis said, "and half when it was all over."

"Well, Lewis," Vernon said, "I'm going to get you another grand in cash money up front, but you're going to have to do something for me."

Lewis was thoughtful. "Vernon, Vernon," he mused. "Not a name you hear that often. Last Vernon I remember was a little kid." He looked around the dark countryside. "Shit," he said. "Excuse me miss."

"Why is everyone treating me like a fragile daisy?" Dolly said.

"You're a Compton, aren't you?" Lewis said.

"I am that," Vernon said.

"Goddam, and excuse me again, miss," Lewis said. "I was a rodeo clown when Otis Compton ran the Crow County Rodeo. I worked this ranch a few seasons, too."

"Great-Grampa," Vernon said.

"So . . . would that make Lyle – no, Frank – your old man?"

"He is," Vernon said.

"Well, I'll be," Lewis said.

Vernon pulled out his phone. "First light in a couple of hours," he said. Pop is up by now, and I'll bet Great-Grampa isn't far behind." He punched the phone.

"Hey, Pop," he said. "Listen, everything is fine, more than fine, really. No problems, I'm fine, sober, and I'm headed your way. Ha! Never thought I'd hear you say that 4:30 was early. I'll be at the house in just a few. Listen, does the name Lewis Billups mean anything to you? Yeah, that's him. Well, it so happens he's with me and I'm going to be bringing him by, and I'm going to ask you and Mom to show him a little Compton hospitality for a few days. No, he's fine, I think" – he looked back at Lewis, who nodded – "he's good, we're all fine, nobody drinking, nobody going to jail. One more person with me I want you to meet.

"Is Great-Grampa up? Do me a favor, it's important – just make sure he's decent to meet someone, okay? I'm not staying long, just going to drop off Lewis and tell you what's up."

5

VERNON RAN IT down for Dolly:

His great-grandfather Otis had come to the area after World War II. He and Vernon's great-grandmother had four boys and two girls. Three of the boys went into ranching on their own; the fourth, the oldest, Vernon's grandfather Lyle, took over his father Otis's spread, the land they were now driving over. But Lyle was not much of a hand for ranching; it wore on him and he died young.

But he lived long enough to suggest that breeding was more his line, and he and Vernon's grandmother – also deceased – produced another clutch of Compton boys, including Vernon's father Frank, who had married Louise. Frank eventually bought out his brothers and some of his uncles' spreads and was now running the ranch. He had also assumed the care of Vernon's great-grandfather Otis, who was still alive and living in the great ranch house with Frank and Louise. His great-grandmother had lived a long life, too, but had passed away a few years ago.

Over the years, the Comptons had bought up other nearby ranches and now owned or controlled close to 95,000 acres, including land leased from the government.

Vernon was Frank and Louise's only child.

6

VERNON, DOLLY, LEWIS Billups, and Frank and Louise Compton sat in the great room of the Compton ranch house. After the greetings and some small talk, Louise headed to the kitchen to make coffee and pull together some snacks. Vernon told them what was going on. Frank Compton listened to all of this with growing amusement.

"No harm done, I guess," he said.

"Not yet," Vernon said. "But I'm not finished with the cream of Iota Tau. Dolly and I still have some work to do. Do you know if Great-Grampa is up?"

"I heard him rattling around down there," Frank said.

"Hang on," Vernon said to Dolly. "Just a few minutes, then we're outta here." He left the room and they heard him call down a first-floor hallway. "Hey, Great-Grampa, hope we didn't get you up."

They couldn't hear the entire response, but it included an irascible *hell no*. Vernon followed an elderly man into the room. He was tall but slightly bent and moved very slowly, supporting his way with a cane. He'd put on jeans and a plaid shirt and – Dolly was somewhat surprised to see – cowboy boots.

"That you, Lewis Billups?" the old man said.

"In the flesh, Mr. Compton."

"What the goddam hell?" the old man said.

Vernon gestured to Dolly to stand. "Great-Grampa," he said. "I'd like you to meet a young lady who is having a little adventure with me tonight getting over on some fraternity boys at the U. It's a long story but we managed to pick up Mr. Billups along the way. She's smarter than anything and she's even shown me the kindness of offering to take me shopping for some college clothes. Even though she's an upperclass sorority lady, she saw I needed a little direction and very generously reached out to me. Ranch-raised, too, and she's not shy about firearms. But mostly, Great-Grampa, what I really want to tell you is that she has fire in her eye and will kick any butt that gets in her way and is up for anything. Great-Grampa Otis, it is my pleasure to present Miss Dolly Ramos."

The old man's filmy eyes brightened. "And a beauty, too," he said, his words soft and slow but clear. "You left that out." The old man held out his hand to shake hers. He held it for a long moment. "Miss Ramos," he said. "Miss Dolly. Vernon, you surprise me with your good judgment, just like your Pop surprised me when he came of age."

Dolly found herself as flattered as she had ever been in her life by Vernon's words. And completely charmed by this old man. And by Frank and Louise, and even by Lewis, but especially by this square-headed clever ranch boy with the lead foot and a vigorous disrespect for the natural order of things.

Otis Compton steadied himself on his cane. "Miss Dolly," he said slowly, with some crust to his words, "we are deeply honored by your visit to Compton Ranch this dark morning and I feel personally privileged to have met you. I can see Vernon wants to get you out of here and I don't blame him, but I hope you will allow him to bring you back to visit with us a greater length sometime soon, perhaps when the sun is shining."

"I would like that, Mr. Compton," Dolly said. "Very much."

"Ramos," the old man said. "Your dad kind of a tough old bird? Big old belly on him? Runs about 750 head on about twenty-five hunnert acres over in Fontaine County? Got hay, too?"

Dolly was startled. "That is my father."

Frank chuckled. "Wouldn't sell out to us," he said. "We remember him."

"Vernon," the old man said, "you bring this young lady back here soon and often and we'll show her how the Comptons can put on a spread. Maybe bring along her cantankerous old man and her charming mother sometime, eh?"

"She'll have a say in that, Great-Grampa," Vernon said.

"I have already accepted Mr. Compton's kind invitation, Vernon," Dolly said. "Now, you do what your Great-Grampa says, you hear me?"

That tickled the old man. His laughter had about it the fog of years, and it ended in a cough.

"And Miss Dolly, I will invite you to please accept my apologies for the foul language," he said. "Mr. Billups's appearance took me a bit by surprise. Two quarters in the swear jar." And he smiled a smile that appeared to disclose every tooth a human being should have.

"Mr. Compton," Dolly said to the old man, "I think I may know what Vernon has in mind for those overbred fraternity boys, and he and I need to get going to kick some of that Greek behind, with my thanks for a most gracious and hospitable reception before sunrise in this lovely home."

"Miss Dolly," the old man said, "the pleasure was ours and we will look forward to getting to know you better, if young Vernon here doesn't f— if young Vernon treats you as you deserve."

7

"WHAT'S NEXT, CLYDE?" Dolly said. "You thinking what I'm thinking?"

"So far," Vernon said, "you and I have not had one different thought."

That was true, Dolly thought. They seemed to be on the same naughty wavelength. She felt that perhaps this was all leading to something good, maybe very good.

Vernon said, "I'm going to say something that Clyde Barrow never said, which is that we've got to find those cops. Sun will be up in around an hour."

"We lost them an hour ago," she said.

"I think they'll still be looking for us," he said. "Pretty sure. It hasn't been that long since we lost them. We'll get back to 43 and cruise around. And listen," he said, "just play along with anything I say. Milk it, baby, but pretend there's an Oscar in it for you. And the no-swear rule is suspended this occasion."

"They couldn't catch us before," she said. "Imagine that."

"They're going to catch us now," he said.

They turned away from town and before too long, they saw the flashing blue and red lights appear and disappear a few hills behind them. Vernon slowed to the speed limit.

"Cops chasing a speeder, and one suspected of a major burglary, are going to catch someone going ninety on 43," Vernon said, "and they're going to call for backup and for help from the other direction, but these cops never did either of those things."

"Because," Dolly said, "they're not cops, are they?"

"Right again, baby."

"And they're not used to driving ninety."

"Double right."

"And they don't want to get pulled over themselves."

"Hat trick," Vernon said. "Or die in a rollover in the top-heavy piece of crap that's pulling up behind us now."

Vernon slowed and pulled over. The chase vehicle, an old Chevy Tahoe fitted with some old-fashioned rotating cop lights, pulled up behind them. Doyle and Bucky and Phil Hatch from the rush committee came up to the Jeep. Vernon pushed the buttons to roll down his and Dolly's windows.

"Surprise!" Doyle said. "Man, you really gave us a run. Where the hell did you go?"

"Dolly!" Bucky said. "The sweetheart of Iota Tau! How did you get roped into this?"

Dolly said, "Vernon here asked if I was up for kicking some Mighty Mastiff ass and I said sure, who wouldn't be?"

"You assholes," Vernon said. "You tellin' me I ran all over Crow County for the last two hours and it was just you jagoffs chasin' us all along? Scared the everlovin' living dinner out of us. Me, anyways."

Dolly noted Vernon's new hick inflections and had to stifle herself.

"Where's the crate?" Phil said.

Dolly interrupted. "That thing scared me to death! I thought sure it was going to bust out of there! That's no mascot, it's a wild animal! It was a mankiller!"

"Shit," Vernon said, "I told you guys I absolutely could not get caught in this. I couldn't just dump the crate out on the side of the road and then get caught down the road – they'd know I'd a-stolen it; that's when I thought you guys were real cops! Look at the splinters and shit on the carpet back there! They wouldn't even need a search warrant, it's in plain sight!"

"Right, right," Phil said. "So where's the –"

"Your story all made sense, you really sold it, Doyle, and

it was working out with the gate and the trailer and Suggs all just like you said. And man, I thought we was home free, Dolly and me, then we're bookin' out 43 high-fivin' each other and I seen your lights back there and I had to think fast. Thank God I know this countryside! And thank God this bus has some horses to spare. So yeah, we ran like hell when we saw you back there! We thought we was dead meat."

"I've never been so scared in my life," Dolly said. "And that goddamned dog barking and growling its head off two feet away. I could hear it chewing on the inside of that crate. I got a little hysterical, didn't I, Vernon?"

"Be honest with you, not sure you were more hysterical than I was," Vernon said. "Kinda glad you guys didn't witness that. We was both hollerin'. I shoulda brought a change of u-trou."

Doyle laughed but there was no mirth in it. "Where'd you stow the crate?" Doyle said. "You said you'd think of a place."

"I had to take a chance to try to lose you – I thought you was cops with one of them big Ford Interceptor engines and it was only a matter of time, so I punched it. Thank God the United States Chrysler Corporation is still making these SRT screamers. And we got far enough ahead that we couldn't see you. We ducked up old CR 14 to the Voyageur Bridge over Big Boar, you know, where the rapids kinda empty into that quieter water where the bass fishermen hang out? Well, maybe you don't, but at the speed we were going it was only about ten minutes up into the foothills. Running high since last week's rains. That goddam dog, when we put that crate over the rail, I swear the thing was screaming."

"I never heard a dog sound like that," Dolly said.

"You dumped the crate in the river?" Doyle said.

"Hey, man," Vernon said, "I didn't want to do it. But I figured if we got caught, think about it! Not just me – Iota Tau was freaking dead! Masterson's in our conference, the dog's owner is a big turd in the county like you said, they coulda had the fraternity kicked off campus! And you told me they were going to give the dog the needle until the owner bribed someone, so I figured, what the hell? I had to do something with it that would separate it from us and make it disappear for a long time, maybe forever. We'd be miles away and have all those splinters and crap cleaned out by the time anyone found the crate and checked the car. You guys were totally on our tail."

"It was my idea," Dolly said.

Vernon glanced at her. "Forget that," he said. "We were headed into the hills and when we saw the signs for Voyageur Bridge, we both said, 'Big Boar gonna take this dog.'"

"Did you happen to notice if the crate was floating?" Bucky said.

"It was real dark," Dolly said. "I didn't see. I didn't hear any more barking after it hit the water, but the river was kinda noisy. The river's high, it wasn't a long drop. Might've floated some."

"I think that mutt sleeps with the largemouth," Vernon said. "You said the dog could get air in there so it wasn't watertight, mighta sank. But I dunno. Crate could have busted when it hit the water and the bastard is wandering the foothills. Or maybe the crate's halfway to the Pacific. No idea. Don't care, as long as it's nowhere near me. And Dolly."

Doyle, Bucky, and Phil were quiet. They were nodding and looking at each other.

Vernon said, "Nice camera you got there, Buck."

Bucky looked down at the big Canon DSLR hanging around his neck. "Uh . . . ."

Doyle jumped in. "We were going to have you take us to the crate and we'd send a picture and directions to Masterson to tell them where to pick up the dog."

Phil caught on. "Proof of life, you know?" he said. "We'd send audio of the barking and all."

Vernon looked at Doyle and Phil a long time with a small smile, like one looks at a liar. "Well," he said quietly, "looks like you boys thought of everything."

"No crate to photograph," Dolly said cheerfully, "but take a picture of Vernon and me. You got a flash on that thing, it'll take in this low light. Then text it to me when you download it. Ha! You've always wanted my number, Bucky." She stood close to Vernon and put her arms around his waist. "Big smile, big man."

Bucky seemed unsure, but Phil gave a little nod. Bucky raised the camera and the flash exploded into the predawn.

"Another, I had my eyes closed," Dolly said.

"I can smile better, too," Vernon said.

Bucky took another.

"Okay, guys," Vernon said, "great prank. Kinda two pranks in one. Masterson's killer mascot is gonzo and you got me with the cop act. Everything went the way you said. I'm sorry about the dog – well, not all that sorry, that dog was a killer, shoulda slept the big sleep a long time ago – but I wasn't going to go down for this, and I told you that so you knew it. So I assume I'm cool with the committee.

Man, you totally sold it! I really thought I had real cops after me."

"After us," Dolly amended.

"Uh," Bucky said, but Doyle and Phil glared him quiet.

"Look," Vernon said, "I'm absolutely beat and I need to get Dolly back to the Pi Sigma house." He started up the Jeep and revved the engine, its godless horses startling the frat team.

"We maybe should go look for the dog," Phil said.

"Be my guest," Vernon said. "Hope none of you had Gravy Train for dinner." He told them how to get to the Voyageur Bridge.

8

"Oh," Dolly said. "Oh. That was cruel."

"Yeah," Vernon said, "but all we did was put a stop to their own cruelty. I almost laughed when I saw that camera. That was going to be the prank's big finale. Those new Canons shoot high-def video. They were going to have me take them to the crate, and then record my reaction when Lewis popped out. There was no way they could have extended the prank past gametime anyway, since we would have seen that the dog was present and accounted for."

Dolly considered the elegant brilliance of Vernon's scheme. No crate and a rational explanation for its disappearance, so no evidence of Vernon victimized by a prank. And a terrifying dilemma for the frat boys.

"Think about it," Vernon said. "They won't find him tonight. They'll be terrified his tiny waterlogged corpse will wash up somewhere and be found by some fishermen.

Lewis has promised not to answer his phone or texts or contact anyone he knows, so Doyle and the boys are going to get bupkis when they try to reach him. They'll have to assume he's dead or missing. Their first choice, their ethical choice, is to report Lewis missing right away and explain to authorities why a fraternity is reporting the disappearance of a former rodeo clown, and a discriminated-against little person to boot, including the possibility of me committing involuntary manslaughter by dumping a crate they themselves had deceptively loaded with said former rodeo clown. Hello, viral media. Bye-bye, Iota Tau.

"But if they don't do that in the next few hours, it gets even better! Since you and I will see Master at the game today, we can confront the entire house board and demand to know who we drowned and threaten all kinds of mayhem. You good for that?"

"Oh, yeah," Dolly said.

"I don't know if I could keep a straight face while I was hollering at them about making me a killer."

"I could," Dolly said. "I can get very indignant about being an accessory."

"Then what do they do?" Vernon continued. "Deny everything? Can't; you and I both saw the thing rocking and making fierce dog sounds; *something* had to be in that crate. And they're out looking right now, so no, they can't say there was nothing in the crate."

Hee-hee hee. "Will they threaten us? Try to bribe us to keep quiet? Will they try to get us to form a pact like something out of a bad movie to keep the regrettable death of Lewis Billups a secret among ourselves to our dying day? What about the undoubtedly unreliable Suggs brothers and unidentified friend? The rest of the frat board? Whoever they got that old Tahoe from, and the cop lights? Whoever Lewis might have told? That's a lot of people to keep quiet for a lot of years and nothing in it for any of them other than a stretch in the pen for aiding and abetting if someone talks. Bye-bye, sleeping at night."

"Do we have to produce Lewis?" Dolly said. "Can't we just keep him hidden forever? He's not very large."

"Even as big-hearted as my family is," Vernon said, "no."

"You got 'em," Dolly said. "You totally turned it around on them. You think they'll forgive you when they find out you pranked them better than they pranked you?"

"No," Vernon said. "And I won't be asking for it. I'm done with those jamokes. But I will make sure they become legends of towering stupidity at Iota Tau and the U. I'll produce Lewis at a particularly mortifying time. Maybe you and I could figure that out."

Dolly said, "I'd be happy to conspire with you on that. How about we sneak Lewis into a Masterson game and have his picture taken with Master. I have friends who work on the U news website and the town paper. I could feed it to them with a story."

"Miss Dolly," Vernon said, slapping the steering wheel, "you are the absolute best." *Hee-hee-hee.*

Dolly figured out how to recline her car seat a little. She laid back and yawned. "An incredible night, Vernon," she said. "Thank you. I know you're a freshman, but you're a special guy. I'm really glad I came over to talk to you. Creased pants and all."

Vernon was quiet, like he didn't quite know how to

respond. "I'm glad you trusted me. You're a cool lady. Really cool."

"We could have a real date sometime," she said. "I don't mean a clothes-shopping date. Forget the crap Greek rules, I'm twenty-one, near twenty-two, I'm ready to be a cougar."

"That would be great," Vernon said like he didn't quite believe what he was hearing. "Yeah, that would be great. I guess we've already got one booked, back at the house, where Great-Grandpa could continue his cross-examination. Hey, listen," he said, "I hope you weren't too creeped out by your reception back there."

"Absolutely not," Dolly said. "I was completely charmed by that speech you gave to your Great-Grandpa. I'm not sure I entirely understood it, it was . . . courtly, kind of old-fashioned. It got to me, Vernon. Thank you for it. I'm going to try to remember to write it down when I get back to the house. I loved your Pop and Mom, too, so welcoming to a stranger, their only son bringing a girl home before sunrise! Somehow, they didn't seem too surprised. I'll have to ask them why."

Hee-hee-hee.

"And your Great-Grampa Otis, what a sweetheart."

"Not so much in his younger days, I've heard," Vernon said. "Then he met my Great-Grandma and . . . things changed for Great-Grandpa. Really, for the Comptons."

"I've been hit on by old men before," she said.

"He wasn't hitting on you," Vernon said.

The sun would be breaking the horizon in a few minutes. Vernon pulled into the parking lot of the Compton School of Animal Husbandry. "Follow me," he said. "It isn't far." He pulled a blanket from the floor of the back seat and draped it over her shoulders. They walked toward the front door of the modern structure and were almost there when she was startled nearly to collide with a bronze statue on a pedestal rising out of the shadows. Vernon got out his phone and turned the flashlight on.

The figure was a little larger than life-size. It was a woman in a simple skirt to the ground and a plain blouse, open at the top with the collar possibly caught by a breeze. Her hair was pulled back into a long ponytail, its end also windblown. The figure was leaning slightly forward, perhaps into the prairie wind. She had a slender bony face with a prominent nose. The sculptor had given her an open-mouthed smile and eyes that saw into the distance and a thin but somehow strong right arm that reached out as if in welcome, or aid. The inscription read:

DARLENE GUNNARSON COMPTON

Beloved Matriarch

"Miss Dolly – Angel of the Ranchlands"

1925-2016

Dolly thought back on the events of the night just ending and the web of relationships Vernon had steered her into, the drama of the dark plains and hills, a reminder of the quiet intelligence of the people of the land she seemed to have forgotten since she had left home for the university. In the chill of the early morning, the campus and the sorority house, once set before her as places of promise, seemed merely full of intrigues and getting one up on your friends.

She suddenly did not want to return, wanted to stay right where she was.

"Great-Grandma?" Dolly said.

Vernon nodded. Tears were running down his face.

"Vernon Compton," she said, "you darling man, this was the best first date in the history of first dates. You kept me up all night, scared me to death, and knocked the snottiest house on campus into next year." And, she thought, reminded her of the romance of the dance of generations on this rough land.

He nodded and sniffed. The big sweet ranch boy was getting himself under control.

Dolly thought about how the future is always unknown, but something always seems to happen in the right here, right now, to guide the next step. No reason to call something a first date unless there's a second. She smiled an inner smile and looked over at Vernon, who had cleared his vision and was looking at her. His eyes held a gentle light.

"Something to tell the great-grandchildren," she said.

The Donor and the Date

1

"DD. JOCELYN HERE."

"Been awhile but you still pop up on my caller ID."

"Sorry it's been so long."

"Hey, I have a phone, I could have called you. We've both been busy, right?"

"You got kids, I got a stray cat I feed," Jocelyn said. "I should have been in better touch."

"We gonna play 'who's most at fault for not calling' or we gonna talk?"

"All right, all right," Jocelyn said. "First, how's the family?"

"Family is almost disgustingly average," DD said. "Darren's out golfing with some buds. Liam, it's all video games and dinosaurs, he knows 'em all. Debating career choices between guitar hero and ninja. We won't get him an electric until he's twelve, so ninja has the inside track. Kelsey just turned an old twelve, so she and I, we're negotiating –"

"Everything," Jocelyn said.

"Everything," DD said. "So hard. Twelve is the new fourteen."

"I was difficult at twelve," Jocelyn said. "And fourteen and seventeen and twenty-three and twenty-seven and up through at least last night at bedtime."

"And God help us," DD said, "Kel's going to be a beauty. She came downstairs to breakfast the other day and Darren and I just looked at each other. Like overnight she turned into this – I don't know what. Baby stunner. We're happy she'll be popular and terrified she'll be too popular. Her grades are great, so far, which weakens my negotiating position. You good?"

"Me good," Jocelyn said. "Health good, job good, stray cat good."

"As thoughtful a person as you are, Joss," DD said, "you didn't call for an update on the family or to deliver a stray cat report."

"No, I did not," Jocelyn said.

"So?"

"I need a date."

"A date. You."

"A date. Me."

"You know lots of guys to date. Frankly, more than social justice would allow. Some women have no dates, but you, the ATM asks you out. Date inequality."

"I'm not that easy," Jocelyn said, "and this is different. I need a date for a function."

"Yeah," DD said, "and I know exactly what function you would expect that date to perform."

"Not that kind of function," Jocelyn said. "It's the Holiday Ball for the Harris County Coalition to End Domestic Violence. Used to be called the Christmas Ball until, you know, can't make other deities feel bad, so long

Santa Jesus. I contribute, volunteer, agreed to be on the board this year. Yikes. Mistake. Good cause, bad politics. But I still have to go to the Ball."

"Why can't you go by yourself?" DD said. "Women go alone to things like that."

"Uh-huh," Jocelyn said. "What do you think when you see a woman alone at a couples function?"

"Oh, I think lots of different little things," DD said, "like *is her date passed out somewhere? Or is she with that woman she's talking to, like with-with? Or man, I thought peasant blouses went out with, you know, peasants. Or I'll bet men are intimidated by her brains and incredibly loud finger-nails-on-chalkboard parrot voice. Or a woman really shouldn't cut her own hair.* Little things like that."

"We really need to get together more often," Jocelyn said, catching her breath after laughing through DD's routine. "Were you a mean girl in high school?"

"Actually, I wasn't," DD said. "But after the last year's-worth of Facebook posts by former friends I've been giving it some thought."

Jocelyn said, "We really shouldn't think like this, should we?"

"No."

"It's inappropriate. It's anti-woman."

"It is."

"It's actually discriminatory."

"Quite actually. We should be ashamed. I'm ashamed I said those things, and you're ashamed you laughed."

"Society's attitude toward women without dates needs to change."

"Agreed."

"Well," Jocelyn said, "it isn't going to change before December tenth, so I still need a date. Maybe things should change, maybe things are changing, but they haven't changed enough – not with the moneyed charity crowd, anyway. You see a woman alone in a sea of couples – sorry, it's just natural to wonder what her deal is. Unfair, but natural. I don't want to be wondered about."

"With your looks I don't think you would have to worry about that."

"I'd worry more. You know, 'gee, why can't Joss, of all people, get a date?' The next day a half-dozen women would call wanting to introduce me to some nephew or son or estate planning lawyer they figure would have to be better than nothing. They would all be wrong."

"Okay, okay, going alone can be uncomfortable," DD said, "and we're jerks for judging women who go to couples things without dates. But why are you calling me? You know lots of single guys."

"Yeah, but they're all like . . . ."

"Completely wrong and awful."

"Yes. Well, not always awful. Some of them are nice, even very nice."

"What's wrong with very nice?"

"Nothing. But it's just not enough. What do they say, 'necessary but not sufficient'? You go out with a guy, and he's nice, and the date is okay, he doesn't say one wrong thing, you don't catch him staring at your chest. But maybe he's boring, maybe he's not so smart, maybe he forgot to check for dog hair on his jacket, maybe you can tell he's trying to avoid telling you he thinks #MeToo is bullshit, maybe you get a look at the check before he can close up the little vinyl folder with the worn-out corners and you can see that he grossly undertipped. But overall there's nothing actually wrong with the guy, he's a perfectly good citizen, he's been pleasant all evening, he'll make someone a good husband and be a good dad, he might even be good-looking, and you never, ever want to see him again."

"Whoo, you are rough. You just expelled from the gender a lot of guys who might have great qualities that would more than offset a little dog hair."

"Yeah, maybe I'm a little judgmental. But if his great qualities don't show up in a five-hour date, I mean, how much more Italian food do I have to eat before I determine they never will?"

"Okay, but this function, it's a one-time thing, really not even a date. You'll be at a big table. You'll hardly have to talk to the guy."

"The problem is that these guys – forgive me for how this is going to sound – they always think the first date was great. Maybe I went out with them twice. Happens, if I wasn't sure the first time. They like me a lot. They're very excited about seeing me again. And they don't waste any time asking me out again, sometimes even before good-night. And you have to be noncommittal in the gentler cases, discouraging in the more aggressive ones. And they try to be upbeat, but they are so sad. It's painful to hear them say 'okay, got it' or 'never hurts to ask' or 'hey, great to make a new friend,' or some other tragic male attempt to deal with female rejection. And then I feel terrible, because they were nice."

"So if you invited one of those guys . . . ."

"Yes," Jocelyn said. "He'd get all encouraged that

maybe I'd changed my mind as I thought back on his rivet-ing account of the time he ran into Don Henley at Whole Foods and I'd have to go through the whole thing again."

"I like Don Henley," DD said. "I might have been riveted."

"Tell me the truth," Jocelyn said. "Do you think this makes me a bad person? I'm not a man-hater, I'm not even that much of a feminist. I just want my life to be interesting and I want my man to be interesting. That's doesn't make me an asshole, does it? I like men and I do want a man and I want to be in love and I want to be married. I do date, right? I'm trying, right? I'm in there slugging away, explor-ing the man-forest. And I don't want to hurt men's feelings, or anyone's feelings."

"No, Joss, you're not a bad person for being particular. We all want someone interesting."

"Thanks, DD. You found Darren, he's great. A lot of my girlfriends married guys who are –"

"Who are what? Special? Really? Special in what way other than that they're nice? But nice isn't good enough for you, you just said."

This gave Jocelyn pause. DD was right. She liked most of her girlfriends' husbands and boyfriends, but they were . . . conventionally nice. Good guys, good husbands and dads so far. Responsible, thoughtful boyfriends. All of which was good, of course it was. But was it enough if you were only going to live and love once?

"But look at Darren," she said. "He paints. He's in that band with his buddies. He cares about the life of the mind."

"He imports high-end bathroom and kitchen fixtures," DD said. "His paintings have been languishing on eBay for months. The name of his band is 'Louie Louie,' if that tells you anything. Life of the mind? It took him six months to get through *Who Moved My Cheese?* Wait, are you calling to suggest that I let Darren escort you?"

"No! I would never!"

"Good. I wouldn't want to hear his answer."

"But you and Darren do seem to know a lot of single men. I thought maybe you might know someone who would, you know . . . ."

"Look good on your arm, use the right fork, not embarrass you with the other board members, watch the wine refills, not stare too obviously at your cleavage in the dress I'm pretty sure you're going to wear, and drive you safely to and from this thing. And then drive away forever."

"That was well put," Jocelyn said.

DD said, "The single men we know were pretty much all at our party last month. You probably met all of them."

"Yeah, yeah," Jocelyn said. "There were some cute guys there, but usually I just talked to them in groups, hard to get a fix. Was there a pilot there?"

"Robert," DD said. "Dating Jane from the party pretty seriously."

"I remember a tall guy with a beautiful speaking voice, great head of hair."

"Winston," DD said. "Gay."

"Hmm," Jocelyn said. "I hadn't thought of that. But you know, that just might . . . ."

"He's a sweet man and brilliant and I adore him and he kind of checks your boxes as an escort, but when he's had too many Stolis, which is always, he gets very talkative and . . . well, gayer and gayer as the night goes on. He's very entertaining, but unpredictable. And you wouldn't want him driving you home. Or getting too friendly with a board member. He slept on our couch after the party. Hold on, Darren's home."

Jocelyn heard her call out to him, *hey, Joss needs a date to a thing who will just be an escort and who will look okay and won't insult her friends and won't fall in love with her if he's told not to.* She heard Darren say something but couldn't make it out.

DD came back on the line. "Did you meet Ben?"

"Doesn't ring a bell," Jocelyn said.

"Quiet but interesting. Smart but doesn't hit you over the head with it. Listener, watcher. Into competitive kayak racing. Nice face, wears clothes. Has hair."

"Wait," Jocelyn said. "I talked to a guy out on your deck. By himself, looking up in the sky. Yeah. Yeah. Kind of remember liking the look. He was polite, I'm thinking. Might have said something about coming from a boat rally of some kind. Don't remember how it came up but I mentioned I drove a Subaru, and he showed me the stars in the sky that's in its logo."

"Gotta be Ben," DD said. "How about him?"

"That's all I remember about him. Pretty cute, pretty nice, pretty better than average."

"That's Ben," DD said. "The pretty average-plus guy you'd hardly remember."

"Perfect," Jocelyn said.

2

"DD! Nice to hear your voice. Really enjoyed your party, thanks for having me."

"You were the only guest to send a thank-you card. I appreciated that and the handwritten note."

"Kind of an old-fashioned guy, I guess," Ben said. "Also, there's a Hallmark two doors down from my building. What's up?"

"Do you remember meeting a woman at the party named Jocelyn?" DD said.

"Jocelyn, Jocelyn . . . no."

"She's very attractive. Tall, brunette, built."

"All of your single female friends are attractive. Also the married ones. I think you must interview them personally for suitability as acquaintances."

"She said she talked to you on the deck."

"Um . . . ."

"You showed her some stars that had to do with her car."

"Oh, yeah. Subaru woman."

"Her name's Jocelyn."

"We didn't talk more than a minute or two. What about her?"

"She needs a date to a charity function."

"I'm sure she didn't think of me."

"Darren actually thought of you."

"He's not my type."

"Ha. He thought maybe you could escort her."

"She's attractive, so why . . . ."

"Oh, you know," DD said.

"She's between guys," Ben said.

"Yeah, something like that."

"And she just needs a placeholder for this event. Some guy who won't embarrass her or like her too much."

"Yes," DD said. "It's not that she didn't like you . . . ."

Ben laughed. "It's that she doesn't like anybody, at least none of the single men she knows right at the moment, right?"

Bull's-eye, DD thought. "Well, not exac –"

"Doesn't matter. It's okay. I've done this a few times, just been the guy with an arm and a tux and a car and a clear understanding that his function is to make her look like a regular guy-dating woman but not make it look like we're a thing and not try to make it a thing. When is it?"

"December tenth."

Ben checked his phone. "Yeah, I can do it."

"Don't you want to know any more about her?" DD said.

"Nah. Is she a zombie or a vampire or succubus or something? Nah. She's your friend, right? That's good enough. Function, her address, time to pick up. Text me the info. Formal?"

"I think so."

"Text me about that. Also, her last name. Cell would be good if I need to text her. She's not expecting me to call, or should I, do you think?"

"Last name Cartwright. I thought you would want to call her."

"But she didn't say I should, did she?"

"Well . . . no."

"Didn't say to give me her number."

"No."

"There you go. No need for us to speak and she'd just as soon not and me too. I'm just the borrowed guy. I know how to be that guy. You can give her my cell," Ben said. "She can call if she wants to interview me or instruct me on avoiding any attempt at acquaintance beyond the necessary minimum for the evening's assignment."

"Don't get the wrong idea," DD said. "She's very nice, super smart. She's a great gal. She just doesn't want this to be like a setup."

Ben laughed. "I'm remembering her a little better. She seemed nice enough in the minute or so we spoke. Maybe even more than attractive. Seemed sharp. Tell you the truth, I was impressed that a hot with money drove a Subaru."

"How did you know she has money?" DD said. "She's usually discreet about that."

"She may be discreet, but not a lot of women wear watches that aren't Fitbits or Apples these days, and I had the feeling that Patek Philippe she was sporting – tastefully, I might add – wasn't a knockoff."

"Ah."

"We might have talked longer, but a couple of women came out on the deck to smoke, so we came back in the house and we got pulled in different directions and we never reconnected. Tell her I know how to be that nothing guy for the evening. And text me event, time, address, tux."

3

"Hey hey, Joss, Ben's good to go."

"What'd he say?"

DD paused. "Not a lot. Said he had escorted single

women for events a few other times. Didn't seem insulted or anything. Actually, he seemed to understand your position. Just wanted the event and the time, your address, whether to wear a tuxedo."

"Did he remember me?" Jocelyn said.

"He did, eventually. He said you didn't talk long."

"Is he going to call?"

"He said he didn't think that was necessary. Do you?"

"I guess not."

"He said he'd be happy to talk if you wanted," DD said.

"That's okay. I guess not."

"Text me pickup time, your address. Wanted your cell in case he had an emergency. I'll pass it along, okay? I'll text you his. Tux, right?"

"Right. Good that he's got one."

"Ben the Boy Scout," DD said. "Always prepared."

4

JOCELYN WAS NOT looking forward to the Holiday Ball for the Harris County Coalition to End Domestic Violence.

She was no poseur. Although she was not under any illusions about what any private organization could do to change millennia of closed-door terror between the sexes, she was sincere in wanting to do what she could to reduce violence between men and women and protect its victims. She had seen it too often among her friends, and even some older couples who had been married a long time. A couple of cousins had not married nice men, and Jocelyn herself had dated a guy who ended up scaring her. She'd had a stalker she got rid of by arranging a visit by some cop friends. And she was shocked when a woman she thought she knew was arrested for knocking her boyfriend out with a cheeseboard when he asked her if she was interested in going to a MAGA rally.

She had not expected to find a different kind of violence when she agreed to join the board. Bickering, backbiting, and bullying among members on almost everything. No topic was too insignificant to avoid provoking a paralyzing controversy among board members with round after round of meetings, emails, gossip, and efforts to recruit her to one position or another. The infighting was exhausting: how to conduct fundraising; whether to fire the executive director or give her a raise; whether to lease and build out new management offices distant from the old main shelter (itself in need of a spruce-up); whether to accept donations from certain businesses claimed to have offended social justice in the past, or perhaps just the other day; even whether to adopt a new logo for the Coalition and what color scheme it should employ. Two of the directors had actually suggested that women and their children coming to a Coalition shelter be charged for the privilege of staying where they would not have the hell beaten out of them.

Some of these turkeys were going to be at her table. She hoped they did not have turkey spouses, but she was not optimistic.

She was also not looking forward to spending the evening with Ben. She didn't even know his last name. Ben the Arm. She managed to irritate herself about this – the guy apparently knew exactly what was required of him, exactly what she wanted, and yet she found herself piqued at his instant acceptance of that role with no apparent interest in her. She even recognized her hypocrisy being piqued that the guy was fine with just being a borrowed body for the evening, as she had specified – and that piqued her, too.

But she did wear the dress DD predicted she would wear: little, black, plungey. Plungey worked with her height and architecture. A diamond-bordered onyx teardrop necklace took some of the attention away from the plunge, and a black Hermès scarf with deep blue and purple accents lent further assistance to keeping viewers' dignity intact.

When the doorbell rang, she tiptoed to the door to avoid clacking on the floor tile and peeped through the peephole. The fisheye view through the smudged little lens was not wholly trustworthy, but it looked to her like:

He was taller than she recalled.

He was better-looking than she recalled from DD's darkened deck. Rather better. Crossing the line over into *handsome*, and the needle on her personal handsome-meter was well into *very handsome* territory.

He had buttoned his tux jacket over a vest with a deep black-on-black pattern. Gold-trimmed black studs on the shirt.

His bowtie was a Christmassy red and green.

He had a smile on his face.

And damned if he wasn't standing well back from the door as though he knew she'd be peeping and he was making it easier for her to check him out top to toe.

All right. Not sure about the bowtie, but all right. Based on this optically fishy inspection, she judged that Ben would be a satisfactory cardboard cutout for the evening.

She opened the door.

"Good evening," he said. "I'm Ben."

"Hi, Ben. I remember," Jocelyn said. "I'm Jocelyn."

"I remember too. Looks like I rang the right doorbell. If I may be permitted one personal observation, you look sensational."

He's not flirting. That's something he always says. This is an okay way to start, he doesn't mean anything.

"Oh, thanks," she said.

Awkward. "And thank you for doing this tonight," she said.

"My pleasure," he said. "I was looking forward to it."

Also something he always says. And so obviously not so.

"Got everything?" he said.

"Uh, yeah."

He laughed. "Sorry. I always ask that. I kind of have a mental checklist for things like this, things to make sure I do and don't do."

Yep, that's what it's feeling like, a checklist.

"You'd be surprised at what people leave behind after they've rushed to get ready. Phones, lipstick, house keys. One was a woman who wore flats for the drive to the party but forgot to bring her heels to change into. I asked that to one woman who ran back into the house and when she came back she was jamming some pepper spray into her purse."

"Think I'm okay." But she did a quick mental inventory of the stuff she transferred into her clutch from her big-girl everyday purse.

Ben said, "Then we're off."

He opened the car door for her.

Jocelyn felt she needed to say something. "This is nice," she said. "Is this a Lexus?"

134 | Raven Easton

"Infiniti."

They buckled in and he headed out of her subdivision. "Do you know where we're going?" Jocelyn said.

"JW Marriott by the Galleria," Ben said. "Checked it online, looks like a great cause. Before I rang the doorbell Google Maps said about forty minutes."

And that appeared to conclude his remarks for the drive.

They rode in silence for several minutes. He concentrated on the road. Did not even glance her way. She tried to look him over more carefully without being too obvious. Yes, this was going to work, at least aesthetically. She would definitely be okay walking into the party with him.

Yep, she concluded. *He's quiet. DD said he was quiet. And now he's just being the arm. Being quiet is on his checklist.*

Just what I wanted.

But it's going to be stupid to sit here for forty minutes not saying anything.

"You know," she said, "I hope DD didn't give you the wrong impression. I know I said I just wanted an escort, and she may have suggested that I – well, that I . . . ."

"That you didn't want the escort to interpret this as a setup or take any particular interest in you. Yes, she was rather explicit about that. And it's completely understood. You will not have that kind of issue with me."

"But it's not like I don't want you to talk to me." That sounded a little more needy than she had intended.

He considered this for a moment, as though perhaps he did think he wasn't supposed to talk to her.

"All right," he said slowly. "What would you like to talk about?"

"No no," she said. "I don't mean that talking to me is like part of the escort assignment, something you have to do."

Another pause. "All right," he said.

"I've confused things, haven't I?" she said, and chuckled.

"I'm not sure if I'm confused, so I guess that means yes, I'm a little confused. I think you mean we should just talk to each other like people who are having a normal conversation."

"Yes," she said.

"One that emerges naturally and organically from neither of us having any idea what to say."

"Yeah." She chuckled a short chuckle. "Something like that."

"Okay," he said. He chuckled too. "I can sound like a normal human being – you know, if the assignment calls for it."

"It does," she said. "Let's be humans, shall we?"

"I might even sound like a male human being from time to time."

"I have definite female tendencies," she said.

"I don't know why I felt it necessary to say that," Ben said.

"I do," Jocelyn said. "It's because, as you said, DD told you I didn't want some guy who was going to think this was a date, and you're trying to be that kind of guy. And now that we've broken the ice a little, you're worried that maybe you won't sound like that kind of guy but will sound more like an interested-in-me type of guy and you'll feel guilty about it."

"You seem to have given the conditions of our

conversation some thought," he said. "I'm not sure I have your preferences sorted out, but whatever. I will try to stay on the ungendered side of human. We still need a topic."

Jocelyn said, "It interested me that DD said you had been an escort a few other times."

"Yeah," he said. "Let me think. I don't remember exactly. Eight or nine? Maybe closer to a dozen, now that I think. That may sound like a lot, but I've been asked to do it since I was in my early twenties so it's not as frequent as it sounds."

"Were they all like me?" Jocelyn said. "A woman who wanted an escort but . . . ." She wasn't sure how to describe what she didn't want.

"But didn't have a particular guy she felt comfortable asking to an affair at that particular time?" Ben said, and Jocelyn nodded. "Yes, most like that, but not all."

"How do you know all these women?"

"Oh," he said, "I don't know them at all, most of the time. I'm not doing it for them, really. I think of it as doing a favor for the person who asked me to do it, which is usually someone like DD, a mutual friend. But a couple of times the woman herself will be an acquaintance and ask me to be a date for something she thinks she needs a date for."

"But not always women like me."

"Right. Sometimes an older woman, maybe a recent widow or divorcee who was not yet comfortable going to a function alone. A couple of times it was even a married woman. One time the husband was a friend of mine who was going to be out of town when there was some affair his wife wanted to attend. Another time I think the husband just didn't want to go to the opera, and they enlisted me to fill his seat."

"Did any of these escortings ever turn into anything?"

"No. Well, sometimes a friendship, which is not nothing, of course."

"None of the women wanted to see you again after meeting you?"

"A couple did. Some."

"But . . . what?"

"You know, they were nice. They were real nice. Just not a fit."

"You're being nice right now, aren't you?" Jocelyn said.

"I always try to be nice," Ben said.

"You know what I mean," she said. "You're trying to avoid saying they may have been single for a reason."

Ben said, "I do not want to be ungallant. Not every man or woman is going to be every other man or woman's type. They just weren't mine."

"Your gallantry is refreshing."

"In other words," Ben said, "my reluctance to talk about some of these women who are great people but perhaps temporarily without man may be behind the times in this day of everyone feeling free to communicate their judgments about other people. About everything, really."

Your times may be coming back, big boy. "I didn't mean that," Jocelyn said. "I didn't mean to imply anything about these women. We're all looking for that right person, right?"

"Yes," he said. "I guess our generation has been raised to think we're each so special, so we're all waiting for someone whose specialness reflects and reinforces our own idea of ourselves."

That's brilliant. And true. And sad. "I'm going to write that down," Jocelyn said.

Ben paused while he changed lanes. "Kind of a rule of mine that I don't get into too much detail about women I've been out with, just like I won't be telling anyone about you. I think the women count on a certain degree of discretion. Some aren't all that happy to be dragging a man along to a function in the first place. They don't mean anything personal against me, but I'm not going to make it worse for them having to haul along some random guy by talking about it after."

Jocelyn felt herself redden a little.

"Just trying to be a gent," he said. "It's their business."

She thought he was going to ask her about why she enlisted a near-stranger to take her to the gala, while they were on the subject. But he quit talking. She sensed this relationship chitchat was taking him on an uncomfortable detour from his escort checklist.

After a few miles, Jocelyn said, "Do a lot of men do this? Escort a woman as a favor or a good deed? Like you do? You know, as opposed to . . . ."

"A gigolo. I don't know," Ben said. "I suppose there must be a demand for one-off guys."

They were quiet for a couple more miles.

"Do we need another topic?" she asked. "Your turn."

He measured his words. "You know, I appreciate you asking me about this, about being this Ken doll who's a safe date for some big night. I don't believe I have ever reflected seriously on the fact that I've done this a fair amount, and you asking me about it is making me do it. So . . . ." He squinted into the road ahead. "Maybe I should stop doing this. Maybe people thinking of me as some kind of nice-guy date has just become a source of flattery to me, but, like most flattery, it is of no real value and in fact misleading to the flattered, who should be focusing on being a better person." He laughed. "Maybe someone worth actually caring about, you know?"

I've never heard a man talk like this about himself.

"Don't overthink it," she said. "It's just a date."

"You're right," he said. "In fact, it's not *even* a date."

Whoa. That was the premise of this particular evening, wasn't it? Not a date. At least not a date date. He has that script down and he's not improvising.

"Sorry," he said, and chuckled under his breath. "I should model pathos on my own time."

"No no," Jocelyn said. "What you said was really interesting."

"And that's a problem," he said, and whisper-chuckled again. And that was all he said.

They cruised silently past a string of glittering new car dealerships.

"What else do you do?" Jocelyn said.

Ben said, "Enough talking by me. I would like to know what you do. I don't believe we got that far at the party."

"I'm a commercial real estate broker," she said.

"I would think that would be a challenge these days, what with working at home, empty buildings, retail going online, and so forth."

"Yes, it is," she said. "Although I must say, I'm kind of enjoying the slowdown so I can do other things."

"Like?"

"Like getting back in shape. Like going to see relatives

and friends. Like cooking. Like watching soaps." She laughed. "Like sleeping in, let's face it. Oh, yeah, I also take care of a stray cat."

"How do you do that?"

"Easy. You put kitty food in some relatively sheltered place, and a day or two later, sometimes three or four, the bowl is empty. You seldom even see the thing. It doesn't even like you, hisses and runs if you appear. Bingo, you've taken care of a stray cat."

"Have you named it?"

"I can't tell the gender," she said. "Since it embodies classic feline characteristics of independence, indifference, selfishness, and unpredictable hostility, I call it Catness."

Ben was stunned into thought. "Utterly generic yet utterly unique," he said, under his breath. "Brilliant. That is, in fact, brilliant."

He took his eyes off the road for the first time and looked at her. "Really," he said. "Don't take this the wrong way, I'm about to pay you a compliment. Naming that cat with an entirely invented quality and an entirely invented word, that's . . . well, that's really very cool." He laughed and checked the road. "'Catness.' I was trying to think of some more fancy way to say it, like 'if Plato had a cat he would have named it 'Catness,' but what's coming to mind is, 'that's really cool.'"

That didn't sound like a checklist reaction.

"Well," she said. "Thank you. I'd never thought of it like that. I was thinking more like, 'this stupid cat provides not a single benefit of pet ownership, it doesn't deserve a name.'"

She waited for him to follow up, but his attention was back on I-45.

"Do you have a cat?" she said.

"No," he said. "When I was in grad school I had a couple of cats, Doug and Mary, and I ended up really liking them, may they rest in peace, but the truth is that I got them because I thought girls liked cats and girls would think it was cool that I was sensitive and all because I had these cats."

"Didn't work?"

"Worked bad," Ben said. "Girls – women, sorry – a lot of them liked the idea of cats, but the reality – cats are supposed to be so clean, right? Well, turns out a cat is only clean in the immediate vicinity of the cat, that is, its own cat body. But it sheds in the house, including on every outfit a woman might own even if the cat is nowhere near it. It craps in the house, pukes in the house, its feces can harbor things women of childbearing years need to avoid, it kicks its litter well clear of its box, and even in the rare cases when it's pretending to be affectionate, it snags clothes like a jumping cholla."

"I have girlfriends who have cats," Jocelyn said, "and they love them to pieces."

"Women are forgiving of their own cats," Ben said. "And I forgave my own because I really loved those guys. So beautiful, so entertaining. But severely deficient in the attracting-women department. The worst was: There was this woman I met I really liked. Really liked. Met her at a bar and we hit it off. Had a date. Went to a nice spot. She started sneezing and eyes watering like crazy. 'Omigod,' she says, 'you have a cat.' Swear to God, I did not have one molecule of cat hair on me, I made sure of that with the sticky roller before I left the house. I had to take her home.

She sat in the back seat with the windows open positively erupting with tears and snot. The end."

"That's a pretty extreme case, though," Jocelyn said.

"There's another extreme," he said. "The crazy cat woman who can't wait to introduce her cats to yours and make a big happy catty family forever. Look out."

Jocelyn knew a woman like that. Would call you up to tell you about some new guy and it was all about how his cat was going to get along with her three. Never heard much more about the guy.

"I must say," Ben said, "I'm now thinking I may get a cat just so I can name it 'Catness.'" He paused and threw her a glance. "Here I am talking again," Ben said. "You're a sly one, Ms. Cartwright, getting people to talk. No wonder you're a sales whiz. So we're going to get back to you. Now, befriending a stray is a nice thing to do, but pretty low-emotional-investment, it sounds like. I thought when I asked about what you did you might say something about your charitable activities."

"Yeah," she said. "I'm on this board."

"'This board'? Don't be modest. It's a great honor and a great cause."

"The cause is great," she said, "but the board isn't. The honor I could do without."

"I'm glad I raised it, then," he said. "I always ask the woman what I need to know about personalities, issues, things to avoid, things to expect at these events." *Checklist.* "So that can be our next topic."

"Must it?" Jocelyn said. "Here's what you need to know: We don't need to stay late. It has nothing to do with you. It's a big board because we have lots of big donors to honor, as you say. And it's nice that they are big donors and there are definitely some sweethearts, very caring people. But some of them – men and women both – they had to have inherited their money. They think they need to have a position on everything and that Jesus would agree with them. I'm surprised they're smart enough to inhale."

"That's a bit harsh, no?" he said, but he smiled and chuckled softly.

"Oh! I – did you –"

"Not offended," he said. "Inherited wealth can certainly retard one's intellectual progress," he said. "It can retard one's everything. I came into pretty nice money early on. My mother and father died before their time, car accident. Both neurosurgeons at Anderson. I was already working, doing pretty well, actually, at Booz Allen. Only child. Between their estate and the life insurance, I didn't need to work anymore to live in comfort, if not in crazy opulence. I went back to work after my bereavement leave and found myself staring at the screen, wondering why. So I quit. Now I get up in the morning and review my investments for about ten minutes, which basically means looking at what the market's likely to do that day, not caring much about the answer, then grabbing my paddle and heading for the lake. When people ask, I tell them my job is 'managing my portfolio.' I haven't made a trade in six months."

"I'm so sorry," she said. "For your loss and for my unfair generalization."

Ben waved her off. "As I said, no offense taken, and you're not wrong about how unearned wealth can distort one's self-image. But not to worry about your colleagues on the board. Watching my mouth is on the escort checklist."

"Please don't," Jocelyn said. "I'm going to leave the board as soon as I can gracefully do so. There's no one there whose –"

"Whose ass you need to kiss," Ben said.

"Basically," she said.

"You still get the mouth-watching benefit with the platinum escort package," he said.

They were quiet again.

He's a good driver. He's been talking slowly, thinks about what he wants to say. Doesn't want to get too into anything, divide his attention. Almost never looks at me. I invited him to talk so he's talking because his job is to do what I want.

He's perfect. DD and Darren knocked it out of the park.

He's shown no interest in my personal life.

Or me.

Except for the cat.

And the board.

Not about relationships past or future.

He's talked some, after I told him to, but he's told me not much.

Not even the kayaking.

Nothing about girlfriends.

But his not-much talking has been interesting.

All of which is what an experienced escort-man might be expected to do.

Started to reveal himself a little, then shut down.

Damn.

He is kind of beautiful. Smart.

A little stiff.

A little sad.

He took the exit from I-45 to I-10. "Be there in a minute. I'll valet, don't worry about your spikes on the asphalt."

"Oh. Thanks."

"Beautiful shoes," he said.

We're back to saying nice things about my outfit.

He pulled up to the entrance and somehow managed to make it around to her door before the valet guy did.

"Arm, hand, or nothing?" he said.

"Arm, I think."

He cocked his elbow at her and gave a little bow. She put her hand in the crook of his arm and they walked into the JW Marriott lobby.

"It is important to convey the illusion of me being someone you actually know," he said, laughing, and smiling and nodding to an older man and woman who had smiled and nodded at the two of them.

We look good together.

"I meant to tell you," she said, "I like the bowtie."

5

THE TEMPERATURE HAD dropped while they were at the Ball. Ben draped his tuxedo jacket over Jocelyn's shoulders as they walked out of the JW Marriott to the valet stand. She shrugged it off with thanks as she got into the car.

He waited for her to arrange herself in the bucket seat and gather her dress away from the car door before he closed it behind her. She reached for the seatbelt a couple of times, snagged it, and after a jab or two, got it clicked in.

She laid her head against the backrest and tried to focus as Ben took care of the valet.

"You didn't drink tonight," she said.

"I don't drink when I'm an arm," he said. "Partly because I'll be driving the lady home, partly to make sure my table talk for the night is appropriate."

"Well, I did," Jocelyn said.

"You're entitled," Ben said. "I'm here to make sure you can do that safely. Your party, your friends, your fun."

"My drinking," she said.

"You didn't have *so* much," Ben said, a little uncertainly. "Are you feeling all right? Perhaps I should have kept an eye –"

"No," she said, "I'm fine. I'm a little high, that's all. Happy high. Coming down, in fact. I'm fine. When I felt the buzz I hit the ice water. So I'm fine. Fine."

"Hold on." He got out of the car and was back in a moment with a bottle of water. "I noticed the valet guys offering these." He twisted it open.

"That is so nice," she said. "I probably am a little dehydrated."

She could see him nodding in the light from the dashboard displays. He got them rolling away from the hotel.

She stretched. "Ow," she said. "God, my ribs hurt."

He turned onto I-610.

"I can't remember the last time I laughed so hard," she said.

She could see him smiling.

"I owe you an apology," she said.

"What?"

"I owe you an apology."

He shook his head. "I have no idea – what on earth are

you talking about. I can assure you you do not owe me an apology. Why in the world –"

"No," she said. "I do."

He looked at her skeptically.

"No," she said. "I'm fine. Look, I'm sitting up straight. Talking clear. Complete sentences." *Buzzed. A little by the wine, maybe more than a little by him.*

"In that case," he said, "you're crazy. You've been a thoroughgoing pleasure tonight. Apology?"

"I was prepared to not like you," she said. "But it was really only because I didn't want to go to this thing. I was thinking this was not going to be fun and in addition to dealing with the jerkos on the board I was going to have to deal with a mostly-strange man."

"Oh, that," Ben said. "I know. That's not apology territory."

"What do you mean, you knew?"

"Pretty clear. I mean, I didn't know about the board jerks and all, but I knew I was just a guy. But that was okay, because I knew I was only there to be just a guy. And when you came to the door, our first few little exchanges – pretty short, pretty dry, not too happy to see me. All right. My job was not to make you happy, just to not make you unhappy. And that seemed to be happening. We made it to the car. We made it down the road. You were cool. And great to look at, which was fun for me. So – no apologies necessary."

"No no no no no no no," Jocelyn said. "You can stop being nice. I was not pleasant to you. I don't think I even smiled at you."

"You didn't," Ben said. "Maybe in your head you were unpleasant. I don't know what you were thinking. But the

back and forth on the ride down – fine, good. Plenty pleasant. You took the initiative to get us talking. Like regular
people, remember?"

Jocelyn kind of remembered.

"My job was, is, to get you there, sit on my ass next to
you and smile at the table, not pick my nose, get you home.
Happened. Happening. So no apologies necessary."

"All right," she said. "You're going to be a gentleman
until the bitter end, I can see. What if I told you that I
wanted you to fight with me about this as part of your
escort checklist for the night? You won't get five stars for the
night on escorts-are-us.com if you don't let me apologize."

Ben laughed and slapped the steering wheel, startling
her.

"Oh, man," he said. "You are too much. All right, all
right. I unnecessarily accept your unnecessary apology.
Now, let's stop arguing about it."

"Ben." She reached and lightly touched his forearm.
"Ben, look at me for a second. We're going straight. There's
hardly any traffic. You can look at me and steer."

He turned to her, glancing from time to time at I-45 as
it disappeared under his wheels.

"I had a wonderful time tonight and it was because
of you."

"Good. I'm very pleased all has gone according to plan."

"No!" she said. "You're not getting what I'm saying.
Having a wonderful time tonight was *not* part of the plan.
The plan, if there was a plan, was to have a *lousy* time but
you changed the plan into a much better plan." *Huh? What
did I just say?* "I didn't have a wonderful time because you
did some job you were supposed to do. I had a wonderful

time because you were – I don't know, incredibly smart and funny. I know those things aren't on your checklist. All right, I have to say it, good-looking, too. And I enjoyed it so, so much."

Ben chuckled his low chuckle. "Actually," he said, "you may be the one who isn't getting it. Consider: Being myself tonight *was* the job I was supposed to do."

"Oh. Oh. You're saying . . . you're –"

"Me. DD and Darren know I'm sort of an old soul, a courtly kind of guy around women. Turns out I'm a natural at guiding a lady through the night who is probably worried about other things and doesn't need a date to worry about. So they knew I could make your evening tolerable pretty much just by dusting off my patent leathers and showing up with a clean car and –"

"Being yourself," Jocelyn said.

"At your service," Ben said.

"Bullshit," she said. "Okay, I'm sorry for that. If you're being a gentleman the least I can do is be a lady."

"You don't think I was myself tonight?" Ben said. "How would you know?"

"Oh," she said. "Oh. I think you were being exactly yourself, but yourself isn't the sweet quiet arm-boy you tried to make me think you are."

"Well," Ben said, "then I think I'm sorry about any false advertising."

Jocelyn said, "I said I had a great time and I meant it. It's not false advertising if you deliver more than advertised."

"I don't know about that," he said. "In fact, I have been wondering if I owe you and any of our tablemates an apology and I think maybe I do."

"You don't," Jocelyn said. "I told you some of the directors were jackasses."

Ben said, "I must say, that table had some characters I'd never encountered before as a volunteer date."

"They looked normal, didn't they?" Jocelyn said.

"Respectable, even distinguished," Ben said.

"Rank idiots," Jocelyn said.

"I don't know that they were idiots," Ben said. "I would prefer knuckleheads, or perhaps chowderheads. Perhaps a little too confident in believing certain wrong things."

Jocelyn said, "Good thing you were there to set 'em straight."

"That's why I should apologize," Ben said. "I was not there to correct the misconceptions of your colleagues."

"I don't remember how why the sky is blue even came up."

"I think Davis's wife was talking about their granddaughter who had asked them why the sky was blue and Davis said he told her it was because the earth is mostly water and it was reflecting the blue ocean. Then Dick said no, it's because the sky is naturally that color, like grass is green and roses are red. Which isn't completely wrong but pointless, because the question is why. So then Dick and Davis started bickering, and Laurie, I think it was, that younger board member, her husband said with great confidence that the sky was blue because oxygen is blue, which he knew because he used it in his anesthesiology practice at Houston Methodist and liquid oxygen is a light blue."

"Is it?"

"Yes, but the atmosphere isn't liquid, and it's only about

a fifth oxygen. The rest is mostly nitrogen and it's a clear liquid and gas. Ever had a wart removed?"

"But Ben, you didn't jump in, you didn't volunteer anything."

Ben said, "Yeah. I mean, it was really quite unnecessary to resolve the question of the blueness of the sky at the table. I must have had a look on my face or something."

"Well, you knew the answer, so why not say it?"

"Because pissing off three other men at the table didn't seem to me to be a really good way to make a good impression on your behalf," Ben said

He has never wavered from his focus on me.

"Okay, but you obviously noticed that after they'd exhausted their ignorance they just kind of turned to you."

"Yeah," he said. "But why do you suppose they did that? Because I'd opened my piehole earlier –"

"Oh," she said, "don't worry about that thing with Mary. I swear to God, can you imagine those men starting some stupid argument about whether Mary was a virgin? Like after centuries of theological debate we were going to resolve it at the table with men who haven't cracked the New Testament in years?"

"I should have just let them keep talking about the Immaculate Conception," he said. "It didn't really make much difference to their arguing."

"And again, you didn't try to involve yourself in their argument at all."

"Nothing needed to be said."

"It was that rooster Davis. He challenged you because he wanted to show up my date in front of me," Jocelyn said. "That preening yardbird has flirted and made inappropriate remarks to me ever since I joined the board, and he wanted to look like the big smarty in front of you, even in front of his poor mouse of a wife. What was it he said?"

"He asked me if I'm Catholic. When I said I wasn't, he said that I probably didn't have any information on the Immaculate Conception."

"Right, that was it. I just about died when you looked at him very calmly and said that the only information you had was that the Roman Catholic doctrine of Immaculate Conception related to the birth of Mary, not Jesus. That look on his face when the table got quiet and his mouse wife showed him something on her phone, no doubt proving your point. Actually, the look on her face was even better."

"Just a little something I happened to know," Ben said.

"Yeah. Davis probably just thought it was a lucky shot. So he tried again to make you look bad in front of me when they were arguing about why the sky was blue and he turns to you and says 'Maybe the professor here knows,' and he pointed a forkful of bad sea bass at you."

"Another thing I picked up somewhere," he said. "Misspent youth."

"Davis, what a jerk." Jocelyn said. "I could barely keep from blowing chardonnay out my nose when I saw his wife and Dick's wife and Laurie all trying to secretly check their phones under the table while Davis had to sit there and pay attention to your blue-sky explanation, or pretend to."

"Well, still," Ben said. "Looking back on it, I should have just made a joke or something and kept my mouth shut about blue skies and the conceptions of biblical figures."

"You kicked his ass twice at his own invitation."

"Kicking the asses of table companions isn't on the

escort checklist, so I feel bad even if you don't, and even if I didn't start it."

"I'll tell you who didn't feel bad," she said, "every woman at the table. Not only did you shut up their gasbag husbands arguing about nothing, at some point during the evening you made it a point to say something charming to each one of them."

"Mm," Ben said.

"Checklist?"

"Sometimes, if the women at the table don't seem to be getting a word in edgewise. I try to draw them in a bit if I can do so . . . ."

"Charmingly."

"Mm."

"You drew them in. They drew me aside in the ladies' room and grilled me."

"I'm sorry," he said. "Exactly the impression you did not want to make."

"Oh," Jocelyn said, "no harm done."

"Mm," he said.

"You don't seem to realize that I approve of your behavior this evening," she said.

"Okay." He nodded his head as if finally understanding. "Good, then."

And god, Ben had been so funny. After he had quieted the stupid arguments with his calm responses, the entire gestalt at the table changed. He had introduced an inclusive warmth to the conversation; the men stopped their one-ups and the dinner settled into comfortable table talk as the waiters seemed always to be hovering to refill the wine glasses. The reds and whites sanded down what little remained of the prickly back-and-forth. Even freakin' Davis lightened up, joking around, talking about his medical exam, said *I asked the doc if I was healthy enough for sexual activity*, and Ben jumped in *doc said yeah, you're healthy enough, you're just not attractive enough*. Dick said *I asked the doc what to do if I had an erection lasting more than four hours* and Ben said *doc said I just saw your bone density scan, it'd be the only hard thing about you*. Davis and Dick laughed the loudest.

Jocelyn was proud this smart quick man was with her. But it was the dance . . . .

Older crowd at the ball. They had a live quartet with a girl singer before the deejay started during dessert. The group did some newer pop, but some of the Great American Songbook, too.

The singer took a break, and the quartet was swinging slow. Ben stood and held out his hand. Jocelyn did not recognize the song. She took his hand and he pulled her lightly to the dance floor. They were the only couple but he put his other hand around her waist and guided her through the cool heartbeat rhythm without a trace of self-consciousness. She had never really learned how to slow-dance, but when she realized he was not going to let them look foolish she relaxed into his lead, and after a few turns raised her head from his shoulder and looked up at him. He was looking at her.

They had attracted the attention of the tables around the dance floor and older couples were rising to join them. Young women demanded the same of their reluctant young men.

"When did you learn to dance?" Jocelyn said.

Ben said, "I've never done this before."

6

THE WOODLANDS AIR was crisp and still. He walked her to the door.

She sensed he was getting ready to turn and leave even though they had not quite yet paused at the doorstep.

"Ben, I'm serious. I was dreading the evening and you turned it all around. I had a great time."

"I'm so pleased. You were fun and smart and lovely."

"Maybe even a little-better-than-great time."

"I'm even more pleased."

He looked at her for a moment as if considering whether there was any more to be said.

He took her right hand in both of his and leaned forward and kissed her lightly on the cheek.

"Good night, Jocelyn."

As he walked back to the car, her mind raced. She wanted to *leave* the evening *somewhere*, not just send him off thinking it was another job well done, another happy manless customer who was relieved the evening's non-date had come to an end.

It needed to become a beginning.

She said: "Ben."

He turned.

"Did we forget something?" he said.

"Yes," she said.

"I'll check the car."

"What we forgot isn't in the car."

"What is it? I'll call the Marriott lost and found," he said. "Maybe tomorrow morning after everything has been cleaned – "

More needfully, more urgently: "Ben."

His puzzlement faded. "Oh," he said, and said it again, "oh."

"Is the escorting over?" she said.

"I believe so," he said.

"All the escorting boxes checked?"

"All except keeping my mouth shut at dinner. And you gave me a pass on that."

"Then get back – then please come back here and kiss me like I think you want to and I'm telling you I want you to," she said. She smiled and took a step towards him. "And none of your shucks-ma'am baloney, cowboy."

Ben's soft grin appeared and grew larger, no longer a checklist smile. He walked slowly back and put his hands on her waist and pulled her up into him and kissed her softly, then hard, on the mouth. When either of them moved to stop the other would demand more.

When they released, Jocelyn said, "Were you lying about the dancing?"

"No," Ben said. "Oh, I'd stumbled around at my proms like we all did, but I'd never done it with a classy dame like you or a feeling like . . . like whatever the feeling was that made me not care if everyone was looking at us."

"Yeah," she said. "I am a dame. What's your last name, sailor?"

"You wouldn't believe me if I told you."

"I told you, no more dragging stuff out of you. Deliver."

"Bass."

"Like . . . Bass Bass, the oil Basses?"

"Way too distant to register," he said. "If I showed up at a family reunion, they'd toss me."

"Right now," she said, "you're not distant anything," and she hopped onto her toes and knocked him against a porch column as she pressed her mouth onto his until that instant a man and woman feel the moment right to pause and look, really look, into one another's eyes and beyond.

"You're coming in," she said. "No. What I meant to say was, 'Please come in for a bit.'"

That smile again.

"A glass of wine is not going to hurt you," she said. "Except in a good way."

"Okay," he said.

"Call me Joss."

"Okay, Joss."

"I've got my own checklist," she said. "It starts with this." She took a chance and pulled on one end of his Christmassy bowtie and the knot dissolved and his collar opened and the red and green silk spilled down onto his shirt.

"I knew it," she said. "The real thing."

The Genius and
the Gymstar

GUS

How COULD I know from such a distance?

The equipment room is huge at the Four Corners Club. It's like a forest of metal bushes clanking and creaking. But that day I could see from, what, maybe 150 feet? – I started to say that I could see her clearly through the thicket of heaving, sweaty bodies and weights and cables and handles, but that would not be correct.

All I could see was color and shape and movement. And gender, obviously. But there was something about that distant figure that transfixed me.

I knew. I knew. Eventually, there was going to come a day when this woman was going to say "yes."

To me.

This day, maybe.

I didn't go to the Four Corners Club to meet women. Not that I didn't need or want to meet women; sure I did. And at my age, always hoping to find the one. It's just that I didn't join the Club for that reason.

I'm not fat and I'm not skinny. I'm not naturally muscular but neither am I a weakling. A few years back I noticed that the junk food pounds were hanging around some, not getting burned off by whatever internal furnace heats things up in one's adolescence. The softness made my shoulders look narrow and my arms flabby and weak. My features and jawline were becoming indistinct.

I'll say this, though: I had a darned fine head of hair. It's red. Very red. Very thick and red. Still with me, too. I happen to like it. Women – unclear. The old-time bias against gingers seems to have abated, and women never say anything negative, really, but sometimes I think they're thinking *what would the kids look like?*

On that last item the chromosomes are going to say what they're going to say, but the rest I could do something about. I joined the Club and worked out regularly at first, then less so, then regularly again for a while, then less so. Then regularly and never went back to less so. A lot of work to get my muscles a little closer to my flesh. Eventually it got me back to baseline healthy-appearing male. And I've stuck with it religiously, which always struck me as kind of an odd metaphor for most things to which it is applied because, for example, I lift a whole lot more often than I go to church.

I did not look to the Club as a social opportunity. I met a couple of guys there in a racquetball league, and sometimes similar schedules resulted in a locker-room friendship or two, but that was about it. I happen to like the best stuff I can afford, and the Four Corners Club is not only the best athletic facility in my smallish city, it offers a restaurant, a bar, and massages and lots of other services I don't use, but it makes me feel good that they're offered. Like living in a nice big house where I don't even use all the rooms, but I like the nice house. And if I'm being honest, which I try to be unless it is terribly inconvenient, it has some snob appeal in this smallish city where it's hard to find things to be snobby about. (I choose to put aside until a later date careful thinking about elitism and the like.) It's the most expensive gym here, which biases the membership towards the better-off, the better-behaved, and, interestingly, the better-looking. The better-looking may not be better-off, or, by instinct, better-behaved, but they want to hang around those whom they believe to be both.

I'm in the "better-off" category. I teach hardware architecture – that's computers, not chainsaws – at the local campus of the state university. In addition to my salary, I'm the sole inventor on seven custom chip-design patents for which I receive royalties when the university licenses them for aerospace and automotive applications. Some consulting on the side, but don't tell the provost.

I wasn't expecting or even hoping to fall in love that day. In fact, I wasn't looking forward to being there at all. Lifting weights whether by dumbbell or machine is hard if you do it right, and boring if you do it right or wrong.

Even if you aren't looking *for* pretty girls, you can at least look *at* them. That's what I do to make the exercise tolerable.

I try to do it non-obviously. But with her, it was not necessary to disguise my gaze. She was half-a-football-field away, so I just stood there and stared.

LILIANA

Why do I come to this gym?

I have a treadmill at home. I have a bench and free-weights. I have a bicycle. I have a stationary bicycle. The streets are safe for jogging.

I don't use the pool. I don't get massages. I don't play tennis or volleyball.

I make my own meals and I eat and drink sensibly. I don't smoke or take drugs.

I have made a few gym-friends but I don't hang much with the women who come here. I don't dislike them. Well, some of them. It's just that I come, I work out, sometimes I shower here and sometimes just duck out and shower at home, and usually keep to myself.

That is, unless someone, usually a guy, is trying to talk to me.

I don't want you to think this is a big problem. I like guys. And by and large, the guys who approach me here are not jerks. Sure, some of them are just friendly and not hitters, but most of the ones who talk to me, or try to, are hitters. Some of them are cute, some really cute. After all, they're here mostly to try to look better for women, and most succeed at least to some degree.

Even among the hitters, most are not jerks, as I said, and I'm not jerky back to them. A friendly chat, some clumsy roundabout suggestion of some kind from him – you'd think after all these centuries, and the critical importance of human reproduction, men would have figured out how to initiate further contact with a woman a little more smoothly, wouldn't you? – and a polite turndown from me. Usually not a big deal, and we can have another nice conversation later, as long as he knows where he stands, which is nowhere other than in his way-too-clean Nike Airs trying to look casual leaning on whatever machine I'm getting ready to use.

I'm sorry. That's mean. They try to be nice and appealing, and sometimes one of them actually is. But if I went out with a guy I met at the gym and decided I didn't want to see him again or things didn't work out, it would be uncomfortable. For some reason, I've never had that special feeling with any of the guys here that would overcome my reluctance to date a guy who probably wouldn't work out, no pun intended, and then have to wipe his sweat off the seat of the shoulder-press machine a week later and even have to talk to him, maybe. And I don't want to stop coming here.

As I think about this: It's not true that I never dated a Four Corners guy. Jacques. I swear, Jacques. He was nice. He was stunning. Not in that order. The major cool thing about him was that he pronounced his name the same way "Jacques" is pronounced in Shakespeare's *As You Like It*, JAY-queez. He was also broke, and not so smart, but every girl I know has had a thing for a dumb-broke-hot guy at one time or another, and he was mine. But it was okay because he couldn't really afford Four Corners and even before we ran out of things to talk about (about two weeks after we started and a week before I wound the thing down), his dues arrearage hit four figures and he was gonzo so I didn't have that awkward encounter-the-sweaty-guy-you-dumped problem.

But I haven't answered the question on why I come to this gym. If I don't need the hardware here or the other services, and I'm not trying to meet someone, and I'm not palsy-walsy with the girls, why do I spend the money and put myself together for it and spend the time driving to and from?

Because, in a way, I'm the jerk. Depending on how you feel about the following:

The fact is, I am attractive. Yeah, yeah, I'm smart, too. (Aren't all us women supposed to be smart these days? Right.) I teach high school English, German, and Spanish. Anyway, I look great; sorry, I really do. I can't bring myself to seriously write *I'm beautiful* or *I'm gorgeous* or other conclusory phrase (although I guess I just did) because it sounds too egotistical. But on whatever scale female beauty is measured, I'm up there.

And when my school day is over and the tests are graded and my fictional lesson plans submitted, I don't want to just be attractive sitting at home all by myself reading a book or watching television. Being attractive is among my chief assets, if not my chiefest one, and the dividend for owning this asset is attracting male attention. Although my self-imposed rule of not dating Four Corners guys means this attention may not result in a relationship, that attention is still very gratifying, very pleasurable to me.

And with today's toys, I can still read my books and watch my shows while I'm on the machines.

And my attractive appearance, especially as that appearance is displayed in motion on the cardio and weight machines, gives pleasure to the guys who see me, and maybe even a dollop of pleasurable hopefulness to the ones who put their own egos on the line to come over and chat me up.

On top of that, I won't always be attractive, or as attractive as I am now. I don't want to waste this asset's useful life sitting at home.

I think of it this way: My attractive appearance when I am out in public is like a display of a work of art, or, maybe more accurately, something from nature that is pleasing to the eye and spirit. My attractive appearance is like an uninterrupted, free broadcast to the particular community that inhabits Four Corners. I enjoy conveying that impression; the men enjoy perceiving it. The women are free to ignore it, so no harm done there.

All of this self-analysis may make me seem weird. Or awful. Or at all events terribly self-absorbed.

But it is true.

It also makes me sound like I don't care about falling in love.

And that is not true.

In the meantime, here I am, staying fit and being seen.

Like by that red-headed guy across the room whose vision is apparently worse than mine.

GUS

I HAVE PRETTY good vision. But what I saw across the room, that woman, it was like I was seeing an idea. Oh, I could tell it was a woman, and I could tell that she was not far from the median of female shapes and sizes, and I could see colors and that her limbs and features were all in the right places, but that was about it.

Correction: I could see her hair.

She had a lot of hair. Black, thick. Over her shoulders, down her back some. And it looked like some of it was swept across her forehead and she's holding it in place with a band, keeping it out of her face, keeping that big lot of hair over her ears and behind her. I didn't know if it was correctly called a sweatband. I didn't envision her sweating. It was maybe braided, chunky? Or maybe just wide.

She was wearing a bright red tank with matching red leggings.

Something else. Her skin. Really, really, white and pale, or maybe it just looked that way because of the black hair. Or because I was seeing it against a smear of red – red top, red legs, and big, bright red lips.

Latina, maybe? All right, good.

It's funny, isn't it, the difference between persons we recognize as beautiful or handsome and those we find plain or unattractive? Take detailed measurements of the facial features of recognized beauties versus the run of generic humans: the distance between eyes, the diameter of nostrils, the thickness of lips, the elevation of the cheekbones, the length and shape of the nose, angle of ear from skull, the retreat of the chin from the mouth – and the differences between the beauty and the generic would be measured in millimeters. Millimeters! Even bustlines on women – empires rise and fall on 34 versus 36, a B versus a D. What is rational about that, and what is fair? Not one thing. I'll tell you right now, you take a tape measure to Harrison Ford's mug and my own and you'd be shocked at the tiny differences. And yet, no one would mistake me for a young Harrison Ford.

A young Henry Ford, maybe.

Not rational or fair. But so it might have been that day that when I was able to get a better fix on her, I would discover that she did not possess one of the thrilling combinations of measurements that, in my imagining, accompanied her color and form.

But you must believe me that it did not matter. I was smitten from the moment I walked into the gym. I can't give you the reason because my attraction to her was beyond reason and beyond as well any typical evaluation of female allure. Charisma, is that what one would call it? An indescribable something that reached across the distance between us and ignored my conventional judgment of beauty like smoke ignores a closed door.

All I knew was, I had to meet her that very day. Not the next time we were both there, not some hokey staged "accidental" encounter as we both left the Club. No. Before we left the room.

I considered my strategy.

I couldn't just sprint across the gym right up to her and start talking. She'd see me coming and either bolt or holler for security, but however it manifested itself, she'd be alarmed. Causing preliminary terror in the object of interest would have been, shall we say, counterindicated.

Therefore, it would have to be something that was either (a) indirect, or (b) took some time. There was really no indirect route to her – she was on an elliptical next to a wall that faced out into the gym, which meant she had eyes on all access routes, so option (a) was out. Option (b) depended on her still being there by the time I'd contrived some way to encounter her. Since I didn't know how long she had been working out when she placed my soul under arrest, I was just going to have to hope that she would stick around a while longer.

There was only one rational course of action. Inconvenient, but at least sincere and potentially productive:

I was going to have to actually work out on machine after machine, taking a route which would, with careful planning but, concededly, some luck, intersect with her own workout plan.

Fingers crossed that she'd be working out long enough to bring me within convincing flirting distance.

LILIANA

HE PROBABLY THOUGHT I wouldn't notice him looking at me.

But guys don't know what it's like to be a woman, especially a pretty woman. We're very accustomed to being looked at by men, and when either the men or the circumstances aren't scary, it isn't a horrible feeling. As I said before – for me, it's pleasurable, up to a point. (Some attractive women may complain about constant male surveillance, but when they don't detect it, they're annoyed.) And it's so constant, we are so very much on display and so very aware of it – we dress for it, make up for it, diet for it, sweat for it – that it's a part of our lives that most of us accept and account for, like having to do laundry or pay bills or get a job. Some women reject these requirements – that's fine. I'm actually a little jealous of that mindset sometimes.

But me, I'm going to play on that hey-guys-look-over-here playing field, at least until that day arrives that I will look ridiculous doing so.

And I'm hoping that by the time that day arrives, I will have secured a nice man, a good man, for my life.

I'm thinking I need to explain myself better here. Feminists talk about "the male gaze," the viewing of women by men as a sexual object, a thing the appearance of which gives them pleasure, as opposed to the gazed-at woman being a person with feelings, talents, brains, and so forth. They disapprove of this. And if that were the only way men and women interacted, I would, too.

It's not. Visual sexual attraction isn't the only thing that brings the sexes together. Men approach women to speak with them, and women increasingly reach out to men. They go on dates, they hang out, they go steady. The forms and behaviors and words have changed over the decades, but the structure has not. The unspoken assumption – that is, sex, somewhere down the road – underlying the getting-to-know-you stuff may relate to the necessities of human reproduction and plain old human craving, but people crave as well the pleasures that accompany mutual admiration and just good old day-to-day human contact.

I do, anyway. I think most women do, and I think most men do.

But it *unavoidably* begins with *looking*, and being *looked at*. That's just the way it is; the best attitude to have is to be aware of it and be ready for the chance that it may lead to something more interesting – even at the gym with all of the potential discomfort I've described.

So: For this guy across the room to look at me, even from a distance – having noticed me, what else was he supposed to do? Dream about what a fabulous personality I must have? Convince himself, without evidence, that I'm not totally stupid?

Avert his eyes after I've gone to all this trouble?

Now, if his jaw had dropped to his chest and he drooled onto a T-shirt reading MY BLOOD TYPE IS BUDWEISER and his eyes spun like pinwheels and he charged me like a syphilitic rhino, then yes – that would have been cause for alarm.

But the guy was wearing a t-shirt that looked like it had some mountains on it, or maybe it was a buffalo. He filled it out pretty nicely. Not show-off guns or anything like that, but a very agreeable attention to tone. Shorts not too baggy, and the thighs emerging from them were long and also showed some machining. In fact, he was kind of long toe to top, which is good because I'm taller than the average bear myself. (Some women say they'll date men shorter than them but don't. I'm one of them.) Shorts had some kind of school logo. Shoes that used to be white but were now gym-gray. No bands or necklaces or sport watch. A good face; he looked happy. If men only understood what a smile does for their appeal. And topped off by nicely styled red, red hair, and lots of it per square inch. Really quite striking. I'd never dated a ginger. No reason. I guess none ever asked me. As long as red-headedness didn't correlate with any mental disorders, I have to say that on looks alone this was a guy who would make my first cut with some looks to spare.

He might have looked my way a little longer than I was used to, but not longer than I was okay with.

And when he'd had his fill and thought his thoughts, he put on his gloves, picked up a towel and squirt bottle, and turned his attention to the machines.

Not too enthusiastically, I thought.

GUS

THE STRATEGY WAS simple and difficult.

Simple because all I had to do was operate the training equipment I had used for many months.

Difficult because lifting weights is a difficult thing to do if you want to lift enough weight, and do it enough times, to build muscle and achieve definition.

But then simple again because those were not my goals for that particular session, so the heck with the amount of weight and number of reps.

But then difficult again because if I selected weights for comfort and she noticed, I'd look hopelessly wimpy and not really there for muscle and definition, but perhaps there for some reason unrelated to bodily improvement.

And difficult also because all of this was in service of a strategy of selecting machines that would vector me into her path. I not only had to work out to make this happen, I had to pick the right engines of torture.

Fortunately, as an engineer, I'm very accustomed to overthinking.

As unimaginative as it seemed, the best course was going to be to load my usual amount of weight and perform the usual number of reps. It was not going to be impressive, but it was at least going be sincere.

The first step on my journey across the gym was the horizontal bench press. In fact, to the extent it was consistent with my overall plan, I was going to try to do upper-body work first, because as between my arms and legs, the former require the greater attention, and my unchallenging weight selection would not be so visible from across the floor.

If, of course, she even cast her eyes my way, which I was hoping she would not until I could finagle our eventual encounter. Although with my blazing coiffure, I'm hard to miss on approach.

Of course, I glanced her way every once in a while to ensure that she had not left the room, and to see – well, two things. First, perhaps a bit of detail on her actual appearance, which I didn't care much about at that point, having already internalized my need to meet her without further evidence. Second, whether anything about her appearance or workout could give me any clues to her personality, interests, or temperament. So maybe I could come up with something to engage her by the time our paths crossed.

Being flat on my back on the chest press, I was unable to discern much.

But I was able to discern that a large man had approached her on the elliptical.

LILIANA

I HAD SEEN this guy at the gym before. Nice-looking, but there were a lot of nice-looking guys at Four Corners. But this guy was big, too. Tall, but also fairly hard without getting ridiculous about it. Some of the guys who hung out there were clearly doing supplements and probably steroids along with their obsessive lifting – didn't they have jobs? – and looked ridiculous with their biceps like the Hulk, chests like Johnny Bravo, and waists like Jessica Rabbit. This guy was serious about his workouts, but he wasn't there just to be seen; he looked like a guy who wanted to look good in clothes and not sicken women of taste. I respected him for that.

Not necessarily enough to look forward to a conversation with him, but here he came. I was nice.

Somewhere along the line, every guy has read an article that says that the best first thing you can say to woman you want to chat up is "hi."

"Hi," he said. He wasn't sure how much to smile, so he smiled an average smile.

"Hi," I said, and did the same.

"How's the workout today?" he said.

"About the same as every day," I said. "Kind of boring, but you've gotta do it. Brought some reading material."

Now at this point, one might think the strategic thinker would ask what I was reading, and you're off to the races on a productive conversation about reading and potential topics of mutual intellectual interest. And one would be right, but this was no strategic thinker, and no intellectual. He focused on the other thing I said.

"Do you come every day?" he asked.

"No, maybe three, four days a week."

"I try to come at least five," he said. "With work it's not always easy."

"Yeah," I said. I wasn't going to rise to that bait. He'd tell me about that work soon enough.

"Do you like these Life Fitness ellipticals better than the Precor ones over there?" he asked.

When I didn't answer right away, he gave a little laugh. "I guess you do or you'd be over on the Precors."

"Sometimes I do the Precors," I said.

"I heard they were going to get rid of the Precors and put in NordicTrack machines," he said.

"Doesn't really make any difference to me," I said. I huffed and puffed some to demonstrate that talking was a little challenging while ellipticizing.

"Yeah," he said. "I don't really do that much cardio. Seems like I walk about five miles a day."

"Wow."

"Yeah," he said. "I'm a sales rep over at Mander Audi, actually a senior sales rep, so I'm on my feet in the showroom and out in the lot talking to customers, trying to close on the customers that the sales guys have been working on."

"Sure," I said. "Who'd want to get on a treadmill after that?"

"Yeah, exactly," he said, nodding a little. "Ever had an Audi?"

"Nah, I have an innie."

Hard to tell if that sailed over his head or whether he was worn out on that particular pun. But since the male-on-the-make would have taken some care to laugh at that,

I assumed he had stopped paying attention and was preparing for his dismount.

"Come on in sometime and ask for Will," he said. "That's me," as if I'd perhaps missed the point. He waited for me to identify myself.

"Wouldn't that deprive some floor sales guy of a commission?" I asked.

"That's very thoughtful of you," he said. "What I'd do would be to steer you to one of those floor guys, a woman if you wanted, and tell him or her in your presence to take good care of you as my personal friend. And they would, although I'd hope they would take good care of everyone. But at least they'd know I had a personal interest in the sales effort. Then, if you were interested in a car, a deal would come back to me for dickering, final pricing, the usual dance."

"Dancing and dickering, eh?" I said.

"Yeah," he said. "Dancing and dickering." We both smiled at the near-naughtiness. "But since we're acquainted you could count on some kind of Four Corners discount. I won't lie, we won't be messing with our profit too much, but Mr. Mander gives us some wiggle room with friends."

"Dancing and dickering and wiggle room," I said. "Mander Audi sounds like a pretty rockin' place."

"It actually matters who you get when you come in, so it would pay you to ask for me, Will. Customers with an innie are eligible for special manufacturer's incentives. Show me and you get an additional dealer incentive." He laughed and moved off. "Enjoy the rest of your workout."

I may have underestimated ol' Will.

That's okay. Car salesman; he'd try again another day.

GUS

I'D MOVED TO the seated chest press in the next row of machines. You could look good on those machines without killing yourself. And since you were upright, you could look around.

I was relieved that the woman's chitchat with the large good-looking guy did not last too long. But I was also relieved that she did speak with him. They had some kind of exchange. She didn't just blow him off.

Which was positive from two standpoints: First, she didn't just blow guys off as a matter of policy. Second, she didn't necessarily entertain extended dialogues with particularly good-looking guys which, I had to admit, this guy was.

But at this distance, I couldn't tell why she had not blown him off right away, and why it looked like she kinda did eventually.

"Hey, Gus," I heard, "hi."

It was a woman I'd met at Four Corners named Patsy. Her name was Patricia, and probably Pat to most, but for some reason I started calling her Patsy or Pats, and she never asked me to call her anything else.

"Hey, Patsy," I said. "What's the haps?"

"Nothing much," she said. "Little cardio, little strength."

"Little hanging out?" I teased.

"You know it! Better here than The Münch," she said, referring to a German-themed saloon near the college.

I liked Patsy. She'd flirted with me a couple of times, but I'd started it when we were waiting for smoothies at the bar. Cute, real cute, down-to-earth, a farm girl who'd seen a lot of animal husbandry down on the farm and was eager to find a guy who'd stick around for the offspring longer than Nitrous, her dad's prize bull.

"Oh, yeah," I said. "We all feel a little more righteous here, don't we? Huffing and puffing and counting calories and pretend miles on the treadmills while we check out the talent."

"Can't deny it," she said. "But really, it's nice to have a place to come to see people where you're also doing some good for yourself."

"I ask myself sometimes how much good I do myself," I said. "I work out, I get a little bigger muscle or two, I get bored, I stop coming, muscles go away."

"It can be boring," she said. "I still like coming. I feel like I'm soaking up good habits just listening to all the clanking and whirring and smelling all the, all the hard work."

I had to laugh. "You had a good image going there until you got to the olfactory element," I said.

"Don't be a wiseguy," she said. "Hey, are you going to do the St. Swithin's Ride this Saturday?"

"Maybe," I said. "Not sure. I never signed up but I guess I could register the morning of. Need a new front tire, you're reminding me I need to pick one up. Heard a forecast?"

"Supposed to be nice," she said. "Cool for the early start. I was going to do the 27-mile route. You wanna ride with me?"

"Sure," I said, "but text me the night before."

"I'll do that," she said, "but don't you wimp out on me, you wusser. You're gonna do that ride with me."

"Yeah yeah, all right, Pats," I laughed. I was flattered,

but cycling 27 miles early on a Saturday morning, moderate hills, was a high price to pay, irrespective of the degree of cuteness.

I got to work on the seated chest press and considered my next move. My Patsy interlude had burned valuable minutes as the woman continued her workout. Hard to tell when she'd be wrapping up and walking out of my life for the day.

LILIANA

THAT CUTE GIRL went up to talk to that guy. They were laughing. Looked like they knew each other. Well, that was a fair indication that the guy was probably not overly strange. And cute girls were okay with him.

I considered whether he was moving my way on purpose. Maybe I was flattering myself, but I thought maybe he was. He wasn't staring at me or anything, but he wasn't alternating upper- and lower-body machines. He was just going to machines that were getting him closer to cardio row here.

And he wasn't spending much time on any of them.

Which reminded me that I'd gone my two miles on the elliptical.

I really hated the stairstepper. It made my legs ache when I was doing nothing more than lifting my own weight with my legs intended by God to do exactly that. I didn't care that much about my calves and quads, but a girl has got to keep those glutes in good shape. A girl who cares about being looked at, anyway, and, as we have established, I was that.

At least until the years, and gravity, do what years and gravity always do to the butt and boobs and cheeks and necks and arms and smooth flesh wherever it's found. At which time a woman had better hope she has a winning personality, or brains, or money, or a good man already. The dolls who think surgery can delay the inevitable end up looking like – well, dolls. Like grinning, unwell ventriloquist dummies with buttcheeks like soccer balls.

So I stepped aboard and started that climb-in-place. Which itself made me feel stupid. Climb, climb, climb, getting nowhere.

I wondered where this sour mood had come from. I usually enjoyed my workouts. Maybe it was that encounter with Will the Audiman. But really, was it? He was kind of okay, maybe a little better than okay. He was nice-looking. He was probably smarter than he seemed at first. He wasn't just a car salesman, he was a senior sales representative, some kind of management career ahead of him. A responsible man. Nothing wrong with him. Some things right with him.

But the more I thought about him, the more I thought: Were the world's Audimen my destiny? I seemed to attract a lot of them. And not a lot of men who were not like Will the Audiman.

Is that where I was going to end up?

Would that have been be so bad?

No. No, probably not.

Probably not.

That guy had moved to the lower-body machines.

That was a buffalo on his T-shirt.

I thought I'd keep rolling with the cardio a little longer.

GUS

GREAT. SHE HAD started doing the stairs, so I probably had at least another ten minutes or so.

I looked a little better on the seated leg press and the leg extension machines. I could select weights that made me look a more like a man of at least average strength. And I was close enough now that her eyes would have to encounter me sooner or later.

As I made my way across the gym, she had come into sharper focus. Her features were more dramatic than I had imagined. Narrow face, planed cheeks, slightly pointed nose. It all worked, it all sloped to her really large and lovely eyes. But again – I really didn't care. Sure, my attraction to her was visual. I'm not trying to make it seem like this was some purely spiritual quest to meet some ethereal idealized beauty. I had seen her from across the gym floor with my eyeballs; it wasn't like I was attracted by her smell or her infectious laugh, if she even had one. As unclear as that distant vision was, there was just something about her whole being – size, shape, color, comportment – that called out to me.

Seeing her more clearly as I lifted and pushed and pulled and rowed my way across the floor did not enhance my strong need to meet her. It just accustomed me to what I hoped to – what I was going to – encounter.

If she was doing cardio, she might head to the treadmills next. There were some fly machines next to them.

LILIANA

I'D HAD ENOUGH of the stairstepper and enough of cardio for the time being.

The seated fly, good for the bustline.

Looked like that guy was going to use it. I thought I would cool down with a slow walk on the treadmill until he'd gone through his sets.

LILIANA AND GUS

LILIANA WATCHED AS Gus sprayed the seat and backrest on the seated fly with his little bottle of disinfectant and wiped them both down, as she had seen him do as he made his way from machine to machine. Then he did something she had not noticed him doing before: He sprayed his towel and wiped off the handgrips.

That, she decided, was going to earn an acknowledgment.

"Thank you," she said. "Hardly anyone actually sanitizes the sitting surfaces both before and after they use a machine, and I don't think I've ever seen anyone clean the hand grips. And you're even wearing gloves."

He didn't look at her right away. "Oh, you're welcome," he said. "It's not really a bother."

A bother, she thought. *That's not a noun you hear very often in America today.*

"Still," she said. "It's a thoughtful practice and I appreciate it."

"Well," Gus said, "you can't be too careful with cooties."

Did he say "cooties"? "Cooties?" she said.

"Yeah," he said. "You know, they had a cooties outbreak at the 24 Hour Fitness over in Maryville."

"Cooties," she said. "I hadn't heard that."

"Oh, yeah," he said. "Started with one guy in his early thirties who collected Star Wars figurines. He'd come in and shed cooties all over the place and pretty soon everyone in gym had cooties. The guys all started arguing about the best superheroes and playing Tony Hawk's Pro Skater and Spider Solitaire on their phones and snapping towels at each other's butts. The women were cutting their hair into bangs and downloading entire Coldplay albums. Some of the more virulent cases took up scrapbooking. The county made the members quarantine in place right there, you couldn't leave. It was like one of those big cruise ships where everyone gets the runs, except with cooties."

"That's amazing," she said. "What finally happened?"

"First thing was, they had to change the name of the place to No Hour Fitness," he said. "Then –"

"Hold on," she said. "I was just going to use that machine you wiped when you were done. Do you have cooties?"

"I was certainly accused of it by all the girls when I was a kid," Gus said. "Some of the boys, too. Certainly by my sister. Thought I overheard my parents discussing the possibility one night when they thought I was asleep. But if I did have cooties I must have been asymptomatic because I turned into a really cool guy."

"Is that right?" Liliana said. She wasn't sure if he was cool or not, but she hadn't heard a line of patter like this since – well, ever.

"My parents – I never got my shots," Gus said.

"Your parents were, what do you call them, anti-vaxxers?" she said.

"No," he said, "Druids."

Good god, she thought. *How long can he keep this up?* "Where do you suppose cooties come from?" she said.

"That's an interesting question," Gus said. "They're not well represented in the fossil record, although they did survive the asteroid strike at the end of the Cretaceous. There is some very intriguing evidence that cooties were rampant among Neanderthal and *Homo erectus* hominids about forty thousand years ago in Europe and parts of Asia, which brought male-female physical contact to almost a complete halt because of their mutual fear of cootie transmission. You can see how that would have a negative effect on maintaining breeding populations, and both groups became extinct, leaving the field open for the evolution of *Homo sapiens*. And here we are."

Why am I listening to this craziness? But there was something compelling in this guy's line of BS. It just seemed to well up out of nowhere, without hesitation and without him smirking at his own cleverness. It wasn't the line of dreary crap she was used to hearing from the guys who contrived to drop hints about their jobs and money and prospects. His blather was interesting, like he was doing standup just for her.

"I'm sorry about the Neanderthals and the *erectus* guys," she said, "but why are cooties still such a problem today, do you think?"

Gus looked around to ensure no one was eavesdropping. He lowered his voice.

"China," he said.

"China!"

"Shhhh. The strain the US is dealing with now, *Cooticus obnoxitoria* – "

"Stop," she said.

"Yep. The most virulent variant of it was developed in a weaponization laboratory in Guangdong Province concentrating on fictional childhood diseases – "

"Stop!"

"—and imported into the United States in shipments of bounce houses that were quality-tested by cootie-positive Chinese children – "

"You can stop!"

"— in the form of COOVID 19."

"Okay, enough!" she said.

Gus stopped. "Well," he said, "I've failed."

"What do you mean?"

"I was trying to make you laugh," Gus said, "but I got nothing."

"Your cootie story is very amusing," she said, "and I was okay playing along as it got more and more ridiculous, but I'm just not a laugher."

He searched her eyes. "That's too bad," he said. "I know it's not theoretically possible to make a perfect thing more perfect, but some laugh lines on that face might require us to revisit that rule."

Well, Liliana thought, *that was rather forward.* But she didn't know whether to be insulted at the implication that she could look better, or flattered that he implied her face was perfect, or amazed that he had intuited why she tried never to laugh.

"I have to ask: Did you make all that up right on the spot?"

"Not quite," Gus said. "The truth is I had hoped to speak with you and while I was struggling with these machines, I was thinking about conversational gambits that might keep your attention. So I kinda put a little dopey narrative together over the last twenty minutes or so."

"Well," she said, "I guess it worked, because we're talking."

It hasn't worked yet, Gus thought, *because we're only talking. Think fast.* "May I ask what you're reading?"

"This is Hesse's *Damien*. I teach ESL, English as a second language, at Foothills Community. Adult courses but also full-time students. I try to keep interest up by using selections from popular works in their native languages and comparing that to the English." She flashed the Kindle reader at him where the gigantic consonant-choked words immediately identified the language. "I think I'll use it this year with the German speakers. Haven't decided between García Márquez and Isabel Allende for the Spanish. The French, hard to teach them anything. I'm thinking maybe a graphic novel."

"Let's see," Gus said. "'Colonel Buendia was facing a firing squad and remembering when his father had taken him to look at ice.' Something like that."

Liliana looked at this unusual man who had just paraphrased the first sentence of *One Hundred Years of Solitude*. "Pretty close," she said. "Gotta say, it's not often you run into an expert on cooties and Latin American literature at the same time."

"It's about all I remember. I'm certainly no expert in

any literature. I did read *Solitude* some years back, I think a girlfriend kept bugging me. But that's a pretty famous opening line. English is barely my first language. I'm impressed you're fluent in four."

"I got tired of teaching high school kids who were forced to take a foreign language and didn't want to be there. So I switched it all up and now I'm teaching English to people who are desperate to learn it, except the French. Well, that's unkind; the French speakers usually already have a fair amount of English, so we actually have a pretty good time in class."

Will she show any interest in what I do? Gus thought.

"What's your line? Actually," she chuckled, "I've heard your line and I can't wait to hear where that all comes from."

"I teach systems design – computer systems – and chip architecture at the university. Also work in the lab, inventing stuff. Some aerospace and military consulting."

"Sounds kind of cloak-and-dagger," she said.

"The cloak is cool," he said. "But they don't trust me with a dagger. I actually managed to cut myself on the cloak."

"But all that Neanderthal and Cretaceous stuff," she said. "You didn't learn that in computer school."

"Right," he said. "The fact is, I probably did have cooties when I was a kid because I read all the science books I could get my hands on and took natural and physical science courses in college along with math and engineering and systems. I've always been curious, and you can take that either way you want."

"Now I'm impressed," she said. "It always makes me mad when people think college is just to learn a trade."

"*Das ist nicht nur nicht richtig; es ist nicht einmal falsch,*" Gus said.

"What?" Liliana said. "Say that again."

"*Das ist nicht nur nicht richtig; es ist nicht einmal falsch.*"

"'That is not only not right,'" she translated the first clause. "Give me that last phrase again."

"*Es ist nicht einmal falsch.* My pronunciation –"

"Your pronunciation is fine," she said "'*Einmal*' is throwing me, but it's placed as an intensifier there. So it's something like 'it is not even false,' or 'not even wrong.' So the whole thing is, 'that is not only not right, it is not even wrong.' Meaning that some idea is so completely off base that to say that it's wrong implies that it even has anything to do with the subject, something like that."

"Exactly," Gus said. "A physicist named Wolfgang Pauli was criticizing some scientist's theory, and he said that. I thought it was cool so I memorized the original. That's how I feel about those people who sneer at higher education." It hadn't been, but it was now. "It never occurred to me that it would find its way into a conversation with a woman at a gym, or really, a woman anywhere."

"So," she said, "*sprichst du Deutsch?*"

"I am sorry to say that you have just now exhausted my entire knowledge of the language," he said.

"By the way," she said. "I don't believe you. I think that's exactly why you memorized that phrase, to impress girls."

Maybe it was, Gus thought. He couldn't remember. If so, it was a pretty lousy pickup strategy, there being very limited potential romantic entrees for enigmatic quotations from German quantum physicists from the early 1900s.

But yes, it was possible that at one time he might have figured it for something that would impress a woman.

Gus perceived that the time had come. She wasn't going to stand there picking up these tenuous conversational threads forever, and she looked like she was getting ready to climb on the treadmill.

"Look," he said, "I might as well just say it. I could just barely make you out when I walked in the gym over there but there was something about you – I had to meet you. I could tell you were remarkable, and probably beautiful in the bargain. You might think this is a line of some kind, but I could tell, or at least I told myself, that you weren't like any of the other women here."

"Oh," Liliana said, a little flattered, because she herself believed this. "What made you think that?"

"It was a little hard to see, but I was pretty sure you were the only woman in here with no ear buds. Which turned out to be right. And I could see that the device you have there is a reader, not a phone, and not a tablet. You were reading a real book. Now it might have been 'Bridget Jones Meets Frankenstein and Abbott and Costello' for all I knew, but that wasn't the vibe I was getting. Can't explain it."

That, Liliana thought, was a singularly precise observation.

"Also," he said, "look around."

She scanned the gym area. "What?" she said.

"You are the only woman here with longer hair that is not in a ponytail or sticking through a scrunchie out the top of your head like Pebbles Flintstone."

"Wow," she said. "Okay."

"Let me get to my I'm-not-weird spiel, although what I just said may have made it too late for that. But I'm

committed, so indulge me for a minute. I'm not a particularly aggressive guy or think that women just can't wait to talk
to me or go out with me, and I'm probably somewhere in the
sixty-five to seventy percent range on the attractiveness scale,
but I told myself I was going to at least speak to you today,
not going to put it off for some other day when I might see
you here, but today, right now, if you were here long enough
for me to figure out how to do that. I'm not strange, I'm not
dangerous, I'm not a loner with seventeen cats –"

"Do you have any cats?"

"One," he said, "but also a dog. And a tropical fish
tank. And all the animals get along, except for the anemones. Are you allergic?"

"Not sure about anemones," she said. "Otherwise, no."

"Anyway, let me wrap up my I'm-not-weird speech, then
you can do whatever it is you're going to do. I'm not weird;
I'm pretty well-known around town in certain law-abiding
circles, got lots of friends, male and female. You can do a
background check on me, and it will come back 'he's just
a plain old guy who does guy stuff and likes women, and
some like him back, and pays his bills and rides his bike.'"

"You're definitely a guy," Liliana said, "but not so old
or so plain."

She had been thinking about how she would handle
the coming suggestion for further socialization. This guy
seemed pretty self-assured and, while she didn't believe herself to be manipulative, she thought she might push back a
little, see if he was as much heart as he was mouth.

"I'm Gus," he said.

Would she offer her name? *I live or die right here*, Gus
thought.

"My name is Liliana," she said. "Friends call me Lily."

"So I should call you . . . ?"

"Lily."

"Making a new friend is always a special occasion," Gus said. "Would you like to get a drink at the bar after your workout?"

"Um . . . thank you, but I don't believe so," she said. "But really, thank you," again, and smiled her second-sweetest smile.

"May I call or text you?"

She paused, pretending to think about it, and smiled her sweetest smile and spoke teasingly. "No, not . . . well, I think probably . . . no, just . . . not."

"Ah," Gus said. "I sense ambivalence! Ambivalence is good! I choose to take it as 'not rejection.' So I'm going to keep talking. And you're still smiling while I'm talking because you know you don't mean 'no,' well, maybe you do, but it's not a full-stop hard-core 'no,' it's the kind of 'no' that really attractive women can say when they're pretty sure the guy isn't going to just slink off with his weight-belt between his legs but will try again, and that assertion of romantic strategic dominance that works because they're so cute kind of turns them on, to say 'no' but mean 'no but try again,' but I'm not going to try again because I haven't stopped trying the first time! I'm hearing this as 'no, not *today*,' because my invitation was only about *today*, not some other time in the future, and thereby I have divined ambivalence about what you're really meaning by 'no.' Uh-huh, uh-huh, look at you, still smiling! Come on, now. You really should meet me after your workout. Forget the drink, how about coffee? I'm getting safer by the minute! And think about this: There will be witnesses, and you can leave in your own car. Your risk is zero! You can escape any time! Ah, but you will not want to, I am confident. I have qualities an educated woman like you would appreciate, but I cannot possibly exhibit them while you're plodding away on these machines, which I can tell you are really not enjoying that much and from which I can instantly liberate you with my generous offer of refreshment! And liberate myself too because I'm pretty sick of pretending to be interested in lifting these god-forsaken weights. Yes, I know I'm groveling, but I don't sound deranged, do I? No, I'm completely rational. I'm only babbling non-stop without a break where you might try to slip in something discouraging because this may be my only chance to say anything at all to you, and I need to get in all my points. I knew cardio would be good for something someday, I can talk a lot with only few, and quick, breaths, so quick you can't interrupt! And here, look what I'm doing now – I am taking a step back away from you so you will know I am aware that some women might find this monologue a little aggressive so I will voluntarily put greater space between us. See how reasonable? See how understanding? Not aggressive, not scary! I'm intending this to be really more in the nature of pleading, doesn't it sound that way to you? Not dangerous, only a little annoying, but rationally annoying, isn't that the vibe you're getting? Yes? Rational? I'm going to take you not answering as a 'yes,' as in *qui tacet consentire videtur*, silence implies consent, which, in fact, yes, I did learn to impress girls. Good, so we're okay with me standing here still talking. Enough about character issues, let me address appearance issues. I came here from the lab and I'll look nice after I shower and change and drag a comb across my head, as the Beatles would say.

Chinos with a crease and a Brooks Brothers button-down, long-sleeved, not short-sleeved like some tech nerds, and – this is a promise – no pocket protector! And I don't want to get ahead of myself, but don't worry about the red hair. From the looks of you your family isn't likely to have been one that kicked the recessive carrot-top gene down the tree, so no chance of ginger babies, and even if a redhead got over the wall somewhere up your line, only a small chance. Now I want you to know that I am absolutely not predicting babies based on one treadmill conversation, but I know, I mean I absolutely *know* that a vision of matchhead infants flickered into your consciousness. See, looka that, you're smiling, and I can see your tummy jiggling, you're giggling! You did think about redheaded babies! I gotta say the best part for me is that you're not dialing 9-1-1. All right, I'm going to wrap this with something that you can't resist, and here it is: If you will join me for a bit after your workout, I will vote for any candidate of your choice in any upcoming election, thus proving that, far from being unprincipled as this offer might make me seem, I am flexible, open-minded, and utterly oblivious to issues of local, regional, or national importance. It should be apparent to you that I am a happy, well-adjusted person almost completely free of opinions that might be repugnant to you, or even a little off-center! And this speech has dried me out, so I'm also a thirsty person. And this is almost certainly going to be my only chance with you, and, as they say in sales seminars, there comes a point where you have to ask for the order. So, in the hopes that I have erased your initial ambivalence, and with the sincere assurance that I will not ever again bloviate nonstop like this, at least not to you, and will, in fact, listen to your own utterances with care and respond appropriately, I ask you one more time, quite possibly, but not promising, the final time: Will you join me at the bar after you're done here?"

Liliana had indeed started to giggle when he was talking about the redtopped babies, and by the time he was done she was struggling to stifle a full-on laugh, at which she failed. She thought of what he said about the laugh lines. His oration had taken her by surprise and she considered her response as Gus waited with mouth slightly open, like a pup waiting for a treat, or who needed air.

Gus turned to a ripped woman in sleek shiny lemon-yellow yoga shorts and a crop top that was more crop than top who had edged close to listen, and who now clapped lightly.

"Did that sound crazy to you?" he asked her.

"A little," the woman said. "But if she won't, I will."

Liliana was laughing and shaking her head. "Rose, meet Gus."

"Hi, Gus," Rose said, and shook his hand.

"Rose."

"You may see it on TV," Rose said, "you may even have dreamed about it happening to you, but I have never, ever, seen a man beg a woman like that for anything, much less a cup of coffee, much less in public. He was actually begging! I have to tell you I got a little jealous hearing it, Lily."

"You should have heard the cooties bit," Liliana said.

"Perhaps I can, someday," Rose said, looking Gus in the eye.

Gus said, "I thought the cootie bit rolled out pretty well, but it proved ineffective to attract Lily's interest."

"Well," Rose said, "Lily here is a tough nut to crack,

and I truly respect her for that. But there are, you know, other nuts in the gym."

Liliana's initial amusement at Rose's flirtation faded into mild alarm.

"Guys try to come up with clever ways to come on," Rose said. "The begging was very direct and, I must say, quite distinctive. And entertaining. Not crazy. Kind of genius, actually."

"Unique, for sure," Liliana said.

Rose said, "A guy more or less confessing his desperate attraction. I wish I could inspire a speech like that. At least from the right guy." Liliana didn't catch the arched eyebrow Rose shot Gus.

"Maybe it will catch on," Liliana said. "Gus here could write an article for GQ or Esquire."

"It was really excellent begging," Rose said. "Amazing extemporaneous good old-fashioned wooing. Gus, if Lily turns you down, I'm headed over to the cable machines. Come on over and I'll turn you down and you can beg me."

"Rose!" Lily said. "How dare you glom on to *my* beggar?"

"Gus is waiting for your answer, so I'll move on," Rose said, laughing. "See you around, Lily. You too, Gus. You're an instant legend." Rose smiled at Gus before she turned away, rather theatrically, Liliana thought. Gus watched as the sleek lemony yoga shorts moved away, memorably.

Liliana powered up the treadmill and began slowly walking, seeming almost to walk away in place, still chuckling.

"I'm done," Gus said. "Possibly in more ways than one. May I save a seat for you?"

He said "recessive" and "bloviate." And "may I."

That Rose, trying to steal my gu—

"Yes," she said.

The Singer and the Stew

1

FOR NICOLE, EVERY flight was like a vacation. No matter how many times she'd served that route, how many times she'd touched down in a particular destination, she always felt the pull of discovery when she set her feet down on the earth away from home.

She told every young man and woman she'd had the occasion to counsel:

Do what you love.

The money will show up.

The world will not let you die.

Heaven help the unfortunate who sneered because she served the skies as a flight attendant.

They'd be skinless within seconds.

2

DALLAS TO LOS Angeles today, Hemisphair Flight 577. Headed to base, home before rush hour.

Nicole enjoyed the minutes before takeoff after the cabin was buckled in. Everyone settled. No one requesting anything, much less demanding some kind of special service or wrestling with an oversized bag they'd managed to lug on.

Sometimes the captain would mumble inaudible greetings to the passengers. But mostly nice and quiet, just the hiss of the air conditioning and the hum of all of the other systems that were about to sing together to get that bird in the air and over the basins and ranges of the desert southwest to the city of the angels.

And in those few minutes of calm, Nicole stood at the front of the plane and checked out the male talent sitting in the aisle seats.

It was also an opportunity for the flight attendants to banter a bit before their safety demonstration in the aisle.

"I know exactly what you're doing," Aliyah said to her.

"Yeah?"

"Haven't you learned your lesson about guys you meet on airplanes?"

"I only married two," Nicole said. "They weren't that bad. Couldn't do any worse than the internet meet markets."

"Tell me about it," Aliyah said. "Even harder for the sistah."

"You should do what I do," Nicole said. "Airline beats online, that's my motto. At least you can keep an eye on them for a couple of hours, see if they can sit still and behave, turn their damned phones off when they're supposed to, not be jerks. There's no harm in looking, and with the full flights since deregulation there's no time for flirting anyway. I joined the airlines out of college to see the world, and men who fly are a big part of the world. I see them, they see me, and sometimes, a little magic."

"And sometimes, a little psychopath," Aliyah said. "They're all strangers. You don't know these guys."

"Not a terrible point," Nicole said, "although every man is a stranger before he's not. And husband number one was a pilot. You know Joe Fentress?"

"That was YOU married Joe Fentress?" Aliyah said. "Legendary stew hound, no offense. We always wondered who snagged his fine ass. I flew Seattle with him several months a couple years back."

"I don't care what you heard," Nicole said. "I did not break up his marriage."

"No," Aliyah said, "the story was that wife number two, who I now learn was you, broke up his engagement to Roslyn the Redhead, speaking of legends, who did break up his first marriage."

"I probably did pry him away from Rosy the Red," Nicole said. "Joe later told me he was grateful for that. Red Roz was lethal, still is. The stories, jeesh. You ever flew with her, you'd believe 'em all."

"I was never in Roslyn's crew," Aliyah said, "but I dead-headed a flight she worked. And when I say she worked it, I mean she really worked it. Oh, she did her job, but man, she had a word for all the men, and when she found one she liked at a window seat, forget it. She'd lean over with his drink and the whole row would get a show. I'm surprised no one ever stuffed a twenty down her blouse."

"Joe was okay," Nicole said. "You might think he wouldn't have been a super reliable husband, with his looks and reputation, but we got on pretty well. I was faithful. I think he was. You could never be sure with Joe."

"A very nice-looking man, for sure," Aliyah said, "and

always very attentive to the crew, I must say. Nothing inappropriate, just always a good word, how's the family, that sort of thing. I heard the rumors but maybe you tamed him."

"Maybe," Nicole said, "or maybe he was discreet. No one ever looked at me funny or avoided talking to me while we were married, so I'm going to assume that I was sufficiently bewitching that he did not feel the need to roam."

"What was the problem?"

"Former Navy," Nicole said. "Absolutely nuts. I don't know what it is about former naval pilots. Genius on the stick, they could fly a Buick. But for some reason there's batch of them, like a cult almost, convinced that the income tax is unconstitutional and that any law that tells them what they have to do, which is every law, is a threat to their God-given freedom. I got tired of the legal fees and interest and penalties but mostly tired of his raving, which would have been tolerable if his arguments weren't so ridiculous it made the flat-earth people look thoughtful. And he was always on the verge of getting indicted."

"Doesn't sound that bad."

"And there were the guns."

"What about them?" Aliyah said, "Javon and I have a couple of guns."

"I didn't think we needed twenty-three for home protection," Nicole said. "And a back-up gas electric generator, and a back-up to that one. And floor-to-ceiling wall-to-wall pantry shelving stocked with nothing but chili, baked beans, freeze-dried chicken, jerky, distilled water, and SPAM. And a can opener. And two forks."

"Yeah," Aliyah said. "I might have moved on from that after a while. Who was number two?"

"Oh," Nicole said, "that was the psychopath. Just kidding. Not a psychopath, just supercute but dumb. Met him on a last flight out from Minneapolis one night, flight wasn't full, some people sleeping, time to kibitz a little with the passengers. I'll say this for him – he taught me something valuable, which is that sex is not enough. He was a dollboy but I had more intelligent conversations with the Maytag. One time when I wanted to talk about babies, I hid his game controller and he took a swing at me. Before I left I put the controller behind the right rear tire of his Jeep."

They were joined by Frederick. "La-la-la ladies," he said, "you ready to fly back to La-La Land?"

"Ready, Freddy," Nicole said. "How you been?"

"Good good," he said. "Always good with a good crew."

A repeated violent crunching sound emerged from the galley. Carolyn, the fourth crew member, was breaking up the ice that had fused from cubes into unusable chunks.

Frederick was right – it was a good crew, although they had only recently begun working together. LAX-based. He and Aliyah and Carolyn always looked sharp; everyone trim; everyone keeping their cool even with the grumpiest travelers. Not all crews were as slick as this one. Like any other profession, there were good attendants, there were mediocre ones. There were bad ones. Some cool and elegant women in their third and even fourth decades of flying, total professionals – a pleasure to share a trip with them. The increasing number of male attendants was also a development Nicole welcomed with enthusiasm. Always shaped-up, good with passengers, good teammates, and it never hurt to have some larger, deeper-voiced humans around to deal with the occasional drunk or celebrity, or someone who thought he was a celebrity, who wouldn't turn off his phone.

Nicole understood that times had changed for women in the workplace. They no longer tolerated being showpieces in the office or in the factory, so it was inevitable that a certain everydayness would creep into the look and attitude of the women who worked the cabins. But it seemed like these days, she was seeing too many unkempt, sullen, and even obese women who, if you pressed them, would confess they were flying for the paycheck, didn't care what passengers thought of them, and didn't enjoy the gig. It irritated Nicole to think that any woman of the glorious skies would let herself go.

Because to Nicole, it wasn't just any job. It was a performance, it was standing over close to 200 seated people for hours a day who looked to you for all manner of direction, assurance, help, those calm and authoritative words over the PA. Someone to give you something resembling a normal human experience at 30,000 feet and 500 miles per hour strapped in way too close to people you didn't know in a fat tube with skinny wings. Some drudge work, sure, some glorified waitressing, as the phrase went, but you were still a star in the eyes of travelers beat up by the demands of airport security and sardine-can seating and rental-car chaos. You could feel the eyes of weary and stressed travelers on you as you and your crewmates walked through the terminal, uniforms crisp, hair in place, scarves that themselves seem ready to catch an elevating breeze, trailing wheeled bags of almost magical compactness, all of it saying *we'll get you where you need to be and we'll be cool doing it*. Nicole wasn't a coffee-tea-or-me gal, but she enjoyed portraying the glamour the profession once seemed to promise both the beat-up businessman and the hopeful young woman who wanted out of Topeka.

At least, Nicole believed, you were a star if you acted like a star and looked like a star. She was always put together. Her whole package, even in the uniform, was always night-on-the-town. She watched her weight. Skin, nails, hair, all frequently and professionally tended. And Hemisphair always had nice uniforms, kept the style up to date. She always wore the skirt, never the slacks, not even in the winter. Made sure the hem kissed the knee. She had the option not to wear the jacket, but she always wore it, even at the expense of somewhat deemphasizing her rather nice bust. She hoisted the clumsiest bags into the overhead like the free weights she worked at the gym.

And she always smiled, and she always meant it.

Nicole resumed her survey of the cabin. She did look the men over, as Aliyah had observed, but the truth was that her review of what a flight had to offer in the man department was more of a hobby than anything else. Hemisphair didn't forbid banter with the passengers, but their training stressed caution in venturing much beyond professional friendliness with strangers with whom one was going to be shut in a sealed cylinder for several hours. But checking out age-appropriate, ringless men gave the crew something to talk about. Even with Frederick.

"How's it look today?" Frederick said.

"Okay," Nicole said. "So-so. The best specimens are in the window seats today, out of range." The aisle seats did offer some candidates: There was a nice head of hair and a clean pressed button-down in 8D, guy came on with only a small leather backpack. A good tan and a tight pullover in 11D, bald, a little older, but seemed quite satisfied with the look. The sandy-haired guy in 12C had a pleasant look, maybe a little soft south of that; he was reading a big book and would look up once in a while, lost in thought. 20C, adorable buzz-cut guy in camo fatigues, too, too young; but hey, she wasn't too proud to play the cougar now and then. Oh-oh, GQ spiky-hair and scruff-beard guy in 18D, so cute! Maybe a little young? Maybe not! Maybe alert Aliyah, or –

"18D," Frederick said.

"No," Nicole said. "Don't say it."

"I think so," Frederick said. "His necklace says DOPE and he's got these low-cut lizard chelsea boots with no socks and he shpritzed enough Boy Chanel this morning to stun a mastodon."

Nicole regretted that 18D was probably not a candidate, but she appreciated Frederick curating the gay passengers for her. She'd been embarrassed in the past by the occasional pointless flirtation.

The jet was rolling to its assigned runway and the crew took their places. Crews considered the flight from DFW to LAX good duty. Three hours-plus was plenty of time for two services, cleanup, and relax in between while dealing with the occasional passenger need.

Over her dozen years of service to Hemisphair, Nicole had identified three distinct groups of passengers. One group was the experienced travelers who could probably have delivered the safety lecture themselves; they tended to settle in quickly, turn off their toys when prompted to do so, and either go to sleep or wait until they could turn on their laptops, which usually featured exotic spreadsheets.

The second group, the largest, was the occasional flyers who didn't even want to think about the single chance in the universe they would be required to strap on an oxygen mask (theirs first, then their gasping kid), leave the plane via the emergency exits in anything other than a screaming frenzy, or untangle the various straps and tubes of that life vest, bright yellow with the flashing light so the sharks could find them in the event of a water landing, or, as they imagined it, *freaking crashing into the water*. They were the teenagers, the preoccupied parents, the men who brought nothing on board to occupy them, and the phone-starers, maybe once-a-year flyers.

Those two groups paid no attention to the crew's presentation. The third, group, very small, looked at the safety cards and watched the attendants – some anxiously, some politely – as they explained the safety features of the aircraft and the careful steps they should take at such time as the flight went all to hell.

Frederick was the purser for the flight and his safety speech was full of clever touches that had not been approved by the Federal Aviation Administration, so his remarks attracted greater than usual attention. He got some laughs and a light round of applause when it was all over.

Nicole performed the safety pantomime with gusto and good spirits from her station forward in the cabin. She would sometimes try to pick up the purser's rhythm and turn the demonstration into a subtle two-step shuffle while she was pointing at doors and cabin lighting and pretending to operate the emergency items, a little something to entertain the troops.

But after twelve years it was all pretty automatic and she was thinking about something else when she noticed the soft, pleasant, sandy-haired man in 12C holding his safety information card and looking at her. He was looking at her *pleasantly*, as though to say *I'm listening, thanks for this very valuable information, and I appreciate the little dance.*

She acknowledged his attention, smiled back at him. And when she did, and spent more than a passing moment on his face, she saw that his soft, pleasant look was something more. There was something good going on behind that look and it illuminated his features into a mature, knowing charm.

And she also saw that he was holding her gaze for a moment. Not looking her over in a flirtatious way, but paying her some additional notice. Noticing what, and why, she couldn't say.

But she thought this: Somebody home and it shows. Nice that he's in an aisle seat. Gonna file that face away for further consideration, cabin service requirements permitting.

With their mutual noticing concluded, the soft pleasant man with the good face replaced the card in the seat back and opened his book.

The crew strapped in and Hemisphair 577 left Dallas/ Fort Worth International behind, made a wide loop to the east, and turned west to Los Angeles.

3

GOOD FLIGHT. MOST flights were good. You'd read about the occasional jackass passenger or entitled first-class asshole or don't-look-at-me celebrity. But Hemisphair was a single-class airline, and most passengers found themselves able to stifle their worst impulses for the privilege of getting halfway across the continent in a couple of hours in a 40-ton vehicle whose ability to stay in the air not a single one of them could explain.

The flight started smoothly, so the crew got the first service going quickly. No problems. Didn't run out of anything. No oddball requests. Some passengers dozed, others had had breakfast and were coffeed out. Only a few ordered alcohol.

Nicole made a mental note to research why what happened next seemed always to happen on flights west out of Dallas. Smooth air to cruising altitude. Sometimes the pilot would issue a reassuring head's-up to the cabin, but sometimes, like that day, without notice –

BANG-shake-shake-shake and keep shaking and *BANG-shake-shake* again, and the plane would seem to fall into a hole in the air and dip a bit to one side or the other as the pilot steadied the beast. Damned clear air turbulence over west Texas and eastern New Mexico. Nicole didn't have to look out any of the little windows to know there was nothing out there and not a cloud in the sky; she could never imagine what confluence of meteorological influences had selected that featureless spot on the earth to shake that clear high desert air six miles up.

The turbulence was not dangerous to the plane, but

could injure an unsecured passenger. The seat-belt chime would chime, people would return to their seats, the pilot would get on the blower and tell everyone that the flights ahead had reported that the condition would last a half-hour or so, and he should be able to turn off the seat belt sign when it was over and until he did thank you for buckling up and keeping your hineys in your seats.

But the suddenness of the tossing and the creaking noises and continued shaking and *damn* you could see the wings kind of flapping a little bit out there, all of it wracked the nerves. Eventually, though, even the infrequent flyers got used to it and understood that the jet was slicing through that thin if inconsistent air as efficiently and safely as before.

There was one population in the cabin, however, who begged to differ.

Babies in a plane, Nicole had noticed, were like smoke detectors in a house. One started to chirp, or, heaven forbid, detect something it was designed to detect, and the others in nearby rooms would hear it and take up the song, every instrument in the place tweeting or screaming and you had no idea to which one you had to haul the damned ladder so you could pry the damned battery out of it and try to figure out how to put in the new damned battery. In the cabin, once one blessed infant started to holler, some group instinct suggested to the others in the herd that something was going on that should jog their anxiety and raise the alarm, and pretty soon they were all yowling.

The babies had been mostly sleeping on this morning flight. No longer. Bangshakytime could not coexist with sleepytime.

Nicole heard a hellacious shriek, followed quickly by another further back in the cabin. Then another one woke up and began to cry, followed by another and another. Five babies, all yelling, and, as Nicole surveyed the scene, none mollified by pacifiers or bottles. None of the mothers were breast-feeding, thank the Lord, so the crew wasn't going to have to deal with that particular sensitivity.

Passengers were usually cool about babies. Babies cry; sometimes even toddlers need a nap and object to the smallest deprivation with a fit. Everyone knows that. There-but-for-the-grace-of-God was the predominant attitude; almost everyone had been a parent, expected to be one, or figured they had probably set up a howl in public themselves at one time or another.

But with the jet continuing to bump along, and holy-mother *five* babies absolutely out of their tiny minds, Nicole noticed some eye-rolls and some dozing passengers looking around to check the sources of the interruption.

Nicole was closest to the first baby to have erupted. A young African-American woman was traveling with a toddler who was buckled into the window seat; the little girl was wriggling and whining a little but generally behaving. The mother was in the middle seat holding the squalling baby and rocking and speaking to him. It looked like a boy, a total doll with fine ringlets and large, liquid eyes when his face wasn't scrunched into a paroxysm of unhappiness. And the mother was pregnant.

Nicole's heart went out to her. She couldn't imagine the hardship in traveling like that. More, there was never anything much the crew could do about a crying baby. They usually didn't cry the entire flight, so the best move was to wait it out. The most any flight attendant could do was to approach the mother – it was always the mother – and ask if there was anything they could do for her, bring her something, and if she was apologetic or looked embarrassed tell her not to worry about it. Maybe offer the stranger next to her a cocktail. Maybe offer her a cocktail.

Nicole took a step toward the woman – and stopped.

The mother and her children were sitting in row 12, seats A and B.

Nicole saw that the soft pleasant man in 12C with whom she had traded noticings earlier had slid his big book under the seat in front of him and was speaking to the mother.

He was smiling and laughing a little and leaning into her so he could speak to her without shouting.

He did not have the slightest reaction to the hell the boy was unleashing inches from his ears.

The mother was smiling back but still distressed at her baby's distress. She looked around, seeming to notice the discomfort it was causing her fellow passengers.

Nicole wanted to speak to the woman, tell her everything was cool, but something about the soft pleasant man told her to hold up.

Suddenly the man reached into the baby bag the mother had on the floor in front of her and pulled out a small rectangle of cloth. He seemed to know what it was for, or at least what he planned to do with it. He put it on his left shoulder and held his arms out, asking with the gesture to take the exploding child.

The mother smiled and shook her head and mouthed *thank you*, but the man did not drop his arms. His mouth was moving but Nicole could not see what he was saying. She could only see that his features remained pleasant and soft, but also that they had taken on some kind of added secret message of persuasion. Maybe *trust me; you'll be right here; you could use a break; your little girl could use some of you right now.*

The mother looked at the man for a long second and let him take the baby.

The baby continued to shriek. Was there something wrong with him? The sound he was making was extraordinary, Nicole thought, even by flying baby standards.

The man didn't flinch. He rested the belly of the baby on his chest, his head on the spit cloth. And the baby was screaming right next to his ear. He patted it on the back.

But . . . it wasn't just any pat. It had a little rhythm to it. *Pum-pum pause, pum, pause; pum-pum pause, pum, pause; pum-pum pause, pum, pause,* the beat unchanging.

And then the soft pleasant man put his mouth against the baby's ear.

His mouth was moving. Was anything coming out? What was he saying that would comfort a baby in a stranger's arms?

And suddenly Nicole understood.

The soft pleasant man was singing.

She could see it in his breathing. She could see his midsection move with his vibrato. She could see his mouth open and stay open and still as he held a note.

He had his mouth close up to the baby's ear, as though to occupy the entire world of his senses.

Nicole was a couple of rows ahead and couldn't hear a thing and couldn't read his lips, but it looked like a slow song.

The baby continued to cry. Everyone's a critic, Nicole thought, but then –

The baby stopped crying. His eyes got big, looking out at the cabin over the man's shoulder. It cried again, then stopped, and again with the big eyes.

The baby pushed away from the man's shoulder for a moment to look at the him. The man leaned forward and twisted his body so the baby could see his mother, who was smiling and cooing at him.

And the baby commenced howling again.

The soft pleasant man returned the baby to his shoulder, and resumed the patting *pum-pum pause, pum, pause,* and continued to sing so, so softly into the little one's ear. A new song this time, Nicole thought.

The baby stopped crying, made the big eyes again, and this time, it seemed like he was really listening, really hearing what the man was pouring into his head, not stopping, a gentle stream of tone and vowels and pitch up and down and that warm male draft washing over his eardrum, and there was nothing else going on in the world, and it was like the little boy was finding this new chorus of sensations really, really *interesting*, and he raised his head one more time to look at the man, and his chubby little neck lost all its conviction. The tiny guy's head banged into the man's shoulder.

Sound asleep.

The man continued to sing for another half-minute or so with the baby conked completely out on his shoulder, still with the *pum-pum pause, pum, pause.* Nicole could hardly believe her next thought, which was that the man's gentle patting was his imitation of the mother's heartbeat.

The soft pleasant man lifted the boy off his shoulder with exquisite gentleness and handed him back to his mother. *Thank you so much*, Nicole could see she was saying. The man said something back to her and they both laughed a little.

The man retrieved the book and found his place. He kept reading as though nothing had happened.

And as though there were not four more infants raising the dead in the crowded cabin.

In her years in the air Nicole had never seen anything like that. She caught herself staring at the soft pleasant man. There was, she thought, a sweetness about him; perhaps the baby could feel it on the man's calm shoulder.

She approached 12C and leaned over him so she could speak without shouting over the jets. "Thank you," she said. "I saw the whole thing. That was amazing."

"Oh," he said. "It was not much. There was a time babies were always sent to the sandman with a lullaby. I don't really know any lullabies, so . . . ." He trailed off and offered nothing further about the lyric he had purred into the boy's ear. He spoke softly, but he was doing something unusual with his voice, bringing it up from somewhere deep; she could understand him clearly over the engines.

"Still and all," Nicole said, because she couldn't think of anything else to say, "thanks so much."

"I don't mind babies crying," the man said, "and I enjoyed doing it." He looked over at the mother, who was looking up at Nicole and smiling.

"Have you done this before?" Nicole asked.

"Not in a plane," the man said.

"That was amazing for sure," the mother said to Nicole.

"I'm gonna take this guy home with me! Maybe . . . ." She jerked her head toward the back of the plane. The other four babies were still threatening a hull breach.

Nicole wasn't the only one who had noticed the man's performance. A woman in 13D touched her sleeve and said, "See if he can deal with some of these other sweethearts."

Not the worst idea Nicole had ever heard. The next vocalist was a few rows back with a young couple. She wasn't sure what she was going to say as she approached them. It appeared this might have been their first flight with their tiny girl. Dad was holding the baby, and mom was plying the diva with a pacifier and a bottle in which the dear had zero interest.

"Excuse me," Nicole said.

"We're so sorry," the mom said. "She was sleeping until we hit the turbulence."

"No problem at all, please don't worry about it," Nicole said. "Babies cry, we all know that. And you might have noticed your baby is not alone."

"Thanks," the dad said. "But we'd like to be good neighbors."

"Absolutely no one is complaining," Nicole said. "But I have an interesting proposition for you. Do you know the baby that was totally shrieking like a banshee up a few rows?"

The couple indicated that they did.

Nicole said, "There's a guy up there who held that baby for just a minute or so and – and, well, he sang to it. And the baby went night-night in no time. You'll notice you can't hear it now."

"Yeah," the dad said, "I can't."

Nicole said, "There's no rule against babies crying. But maybe he could send your little sweetie to slumberland. I have the authority granted me by no one in particular to let one of you unbuckle your seat belt and bring your little girl forward a few rows. Let me check with him first." Mom was uncertain; dad said *sounds great!*

Nicole made her way back to 12C.

"Sir," she said as he looked up from his book, "I'm so sorry to bother you, but would you be willing to sing to a little girl a few rows back? Her mother or father will bring her here, you don't have to do a thing." She thought again: This is not a bad-looking man, if a little soft.

The soft pleasant man seemed startled to see Nicole's face appearing over his right shoulder. "Oh, hi. Um – yeah, sure. If they have a spit cloth, bring one with. If not, no big deal. This thing" — he gestured to his shirt – "headed for the wash this afternoon, so . . . whatever."

Nicole was afraid that baby number two would wake up baby number one, but number two wasn't broadcasting at the volume of the searing screams of number one, now conked out in his mother's arms. That one continued his dreams of whatever the soft pleasant man had suggested with his crooning.

The soft pleasant man took the baby from the father and put it up to his right shoulder this time. He began immediately to pat the child – *pum-pum pause, pum, pause* – and sing into her ear.

Nicole was dying to know what he was singing. She'd ask him later. She thought about perhaps speaking to him when he was done with baby two, but on reflection thought that a normal ground-based conversation might be more

. . . enjoyable. The roar of the jets would drown out anything other than a near-shout mid-flight. She was beginning to have in mind something more, ah, conversational.

The little girl was less of a challenge than the first baby. The man held her so that she could see her daddy while he sang and patted her back, *pum-pum pause*. Whatever he was singing was to her liking because she almost immediately stopped crying. She issued the same startled but inquisitive stare as baby number one as the man sang into her ear. Unlike baby one, she had no interest in who was inserting these new sounds into her head and she did not raise her head to check him out before she closed her eyes and resumed her morning nap against the man's shoulder.

The man ended his song and moved his hands away from the baby. The dad said *incredible, thanks.* He picked up his little girl and returned to his wife.

Hemisphair 577 continued to bump and roll. The three remaining howlers were having none of it.

Nicole didn't have a particular get-to-know-you gambit in mind but was about to speak to the man again when Carolyn came up behind her. "I'm hearing some interesting things," she said. "Like we've got a baby whisperer on board or something."

Aliyah joined them. "I saw you react on that first baby," she said to Nicole, "so I snuck up behind you to watch. I saw all of the second baby. That guy has some kind of magic touch."

The plane pitched up, then down. The cockpit advised the flight attendants to take their seats. Three babies still going nuts. The first two – whatever they heard from the soft pleasant man in 12C, it overcame the dance of the jet's continued uneven path into central New Mexico, and they slept.

Before too long the air evened out and the attendants all unbuckled and tended to the call buttons. The man in 12C had closed his eyes and folded his arms against the chill of the cabin.

Nicole almost laughed as she gagged in too much Boy Chanel rising out of 18D, per Frederick's warning. She reached up and turned off the call button light in row 23 right when the baby in the lap of its mother in the middle seat erupted into another piteous screech. "I'm sorry about the baby," the mother said, "and I'm sorry to bother you with the button, but that dad over there" – she gestured to the second baby's father – "told us about the guy who calmed their little girl down and also another one. We've tried everything with this one but she just won't be consoled. We're driving everyone crazy and she's driving us crazy, too."

The father on the aisle said, "We'll try anything." He gestured to an older man in the window seat. "Our poor neighbor here is a saint."

Windowman smiled and gestured dismissively. "It's all right," he said. "Babies gonna cry. I used to be one, hard to believe."

"A minute," Nicole said.

She returned to 12C. "Excuse me, sir," she said. The soft pleasant man opened his eyes. He showed no surprise and was instantly pleasant.

"Hello again, Nicole," he said.

She was startled to hear him say her name; passengers rarely used it but it was right there on that little brass tag with the two half-globes on either side. She felt a tiny tingle of familiarity. She liked the sound of it coming out of wherever in his broad chest his voice began.

"I hate to put you to work," she said, "but could you please help us out with another cryer back there? The pilot's going to turn the seat belt sign off in a minute so you can come with me now. It's okay."

She felt the soft pleasant man would oblige, but was still pleased and a little – maybe more than pleased when she heard him say in that soft but bell-clear voice, "Whatever you need, Nicole." *My name. Whatever I need.* He unclicked his belt and stood up.

Then Nicole saw that the soft pleasant man was not soft at all. He was big. Tall; not slender, but solid, not pudgy as she had pictured him. He only looked soft because that large body had to curl back on itself to get into the ungenerous airline seat. When he stood and raised his head – she'd mostly seen him with his face cocked toward the little ones and scrunched down into his chest from the too-small seat and bent into his book – the softness fell from his cheeks and chin and she saw that his pleasant look wasn't just an expression of a temporary internal ease, but was what he looked like. He was not just feeling pleasant in his seat on this flight; he was a pleasant man. His shirttail had come out from his contortions to get into and out of the seat, and he took a moment to tuck it back into his jeans. Nope, Nicole thought, no softness in that belly, in those thighs, in that face, in anywhere. 12C was a solid piece of work, and that was not a bad thing, not a bad thing at all.

He followed her back to row 23. Dad already had the spit-cloth ready to hand up to him, and mom kept saying *we're sorry, we're so sorry* as mom handed the unhappy child to dad, and 12C leaned over to take her.

Nicole saw that his hands were enormous. At first she thought they looked big because the babies were so small. Wrong; those were some big bear paws on that man, but he picked up the little girl and held her like she was a bubble.

The baby was bald and was wrapped in a white blanket. But the man said, "She's a girl?"

Her parents nodded.

"She's beautiful," the man said.

He straightened and began the *pum-pum pause, pum, pause* as he jostled the very small girl into place against his shoulder.

He began to sway. He didn't look at anyone or, it seemed, anything. His eyes were distant; Nicole thought she detected a spot of mist in them. He gave no sign that he had become the object of attention to the passengers up and down the aisle. His mouth was so close to the baby's ear that it was hard to see if it was moving, but something was coming out because in less than a minute, the baby interrupted her crying to stare out at the cabin with the same startled look as the others. 12C turned so the baby could see her parents. More crying, and another pause to give further consideration to what she was hearing. Then more crying, but there was no sincerity in it, the tears were gone. The crying stopped and did not resume, and she closed her eyes.

The father reached up for the baby, but 12C held up a hand in pause as he continued his song, making sure she had finished her concerto. When she continued to sleep, the man lifted his face from her ear. He smiled and bent to return her to her parents.

Crying baby four was in her mother's arms. She had come down the aisle from the rear of the plane to stand near Nicole and 12C, waiting her turn after baby three had succumbed to the man's melody. A tiny woman, her face was smiling and hopeful as she looked up at the man through the wrap of the hijab.

"Mine, please?" she said. "Thank you, thank you."

12C looked back into the cabin and spotted the father, who did not look pleased, two rows from the end. He raised his eyebrows toward the father in inquiry. The father nodded back, his approval less than enthusiastic, but clear enough. 12C took the bellowing infant and put it to his shoulder without benefit of spit-cloth.

"A fine son," he said to the woman.

"Yes, our first, a fine son, thank you."

"We're wearing you out," Nicole said.

12C smiled and shook his head. "I just hope it keeps working," he said. "Middle Eastern scales are very different, so he might not like my selection."

It worked quickly on the Muslim infant. Swaying, *pum-pum pause, pum, pause*, the man's near-sad gaze into nothing, some slow melody breathed into the tiny boy's dreams. He stopped crying almost immediately. It took him a little longer to drop off, but his eyelids eventually began to flutter and he laid his head on the man's shoulder, zoned completely out, drool-free.

"Thank you so much, blessings," the mother said, bowing ever so slightly to the pleasant man from 12C. "Thank you, thank you."

He tipped his head towards her and said, "You're welcome. I guess nigh-nigh songs are universal."

Nicole became aware she had moved close to the pleasant singing man. She liked the feeling.

They watched the mother return to her seat. The father unsmilingly mouthed *thank you* and 12C blinked slowly and tipped his head in acknowledgement.

Nicole thought: I wonder if anyone is recording this. I wonder what I look like as I stare at this guy.

I wonder what we look like together.

I wonder if we look like the way I feel.

The last cryer was up front in 5F. A well-dressed, older mother in the window seat was holding the tiny boy tightly. She tried to shush him, tried to give him a pacifier, a bottle, no good. He was crying, truly unhappy, and sometimes screaming.

Aliyah leaned in and spoke to the woman about the man who sang to the other babies. Would she like —?

The woman shook her head and said *no* and held the screamer even more tightly.

"May I bring you anything?" Aliyah asked.

"No," the woman said.

The man in the middle seat had been quiet and looking into the back of the seat in front of him, but now he spoke to the mother. "Look, Eileen," he said, "Todd's the last kid crying on this plane and they're telling us this guy got all the rest of them to stop and hit the sack. You could hear those babies switching off back there one by one. It can't hurt."

"No," she said. "I'll get him to stop."

"He's been crying for a half-hour nonstop."

"He'll cry himself out," she said.

"Either he will, or I will," the man said.

"It's all right," Aliyah said. "There are rules against smoking but none against crying. If you change your mind, just hit your call button and let me know. He'll come down here if you'd like."

12C had returned to his seat and folded himself into it. He picked up his big book and continued to read.

Nicole knelt next to him. "Excuse me again," she said, looking up at him from her crouch. "I know it's only about noon Dallas time, but you've got about a half-dozen people back there all wanting to buy you a cocktail. May I bring you something to drink?"

The man smiled. "No, thank you," he said, raising his voice over the engines. "Please thank all the people who offered." He turned around to look back up toward the back of the plane. Several people waved to him, and he waved back and nodded his thanks.

"Only one left," Nicole said.

"That one," the man said. "Different. The cry, it's different." He looked forward into the cabin with concern. "Something about it."

Nicole noticed Aliyah speaking to the couple with the last crying baby. Aliyah straightened from the conversation and walked back to Nicole and the man.

"Mom says no," Aliyah said.

"Too bad," Nicole said.

"Okay," the man said.

"Anyway, thank you for all you've done," Nicole said.

"The pleasure was entirely mine," the man said.

Not entirely yours, Nicole thought.

"Thank you, Nicole," he said, and again she felt that

tiny thrill at hearing him say her name. "You have been – well, just thank you."

Nicole wondered what she had been, and why he had thanked her.

Nicole and Aliyah returned to the galley to prepare for the final service. Baby five continued to howl.

"I wonder what his story is," Nicole said.

"Maybe he doesn't have a story," Aliyah said.

Nicole said, "Everyone has a story. Some are more interesting than others, but everyone's got a little drama, even if it's one they've made up."

"He does seem to know his babies."

"Yeah, but how? There's your story. What do you think he's singing?"

"Don't know," Aliyah said. "I'm not a lip reader, but I'm guessing it's not 'It's Hard Out Here for a Pimp.'"

They saw the father from 5E stand and excuse himself as he scootched by the woman in 5D. He was holding the bawling baby Todd. The pleasant man watched the father approach, and their eyes met.

The man in 12C didn't wait for him. He unbuckled and stood.

Nicole watched as much of their exchange as she could as they prepared the cart. 12C had taken the baby but he was speaking to the father. His pleasant expression was overcast with concern. He looked down at the baby as he spoke to the father. The father stood by as the big man stopped speaking and began to sway, and his big hands gently began the *pum-pum pause, pum, pause, pum-pum pause, pum, pause.*

The man seemed to be singing a faster song this time.

He took deeper breaths; his musical message to the little guy seemed louder and more insistent, although nothing could be heard over Todd's own screaming, an unearthly howl that challenged the roaring engines. The man turned so Todd could see his father.

But none of it, not the song, not the rhythm of 12C's caress, and not daddy's face, was more compelling to Todd than whatever was inspiring his tantrum.

By now, most of the cabin had taken an interest in 12C's performance – although, Nicole thought, he's not performing. He's just doing something that needs doing. With this little bundle of misery he somehow knew he needed to do this one standing, maybe to take those deep breaths for this particular challenge that would be hard come by scrunched into the airline seat.

The man's private song continued, but now and then he would slowly shake his head and look at the father. After another minute, dad reached out to take Todd back, but froze when the baby stopped with a cough and opened his eyes to stare. Todd hiccupped twice, burped dramatically, and even issued a tiny smile at his own gassy noisemaking. He sighed and closed his eyes in silence against the big man's shoulder.

The man held the baby for another minute, humming and listening and feeling for his breathing to assure himself that his slumber would last. The father spoke to the pleasant man again as he took Todd back; 12C nodded *sure, no problem*, but gave the father a *think about what I said* look, which the father silently acknowledged with a nod, *appreciate the thoughts*.

Nicole met the father at row 5 as he prepared to return to his seat.

"Oh," she said, "your baby is just adorable. I hope he can get a little more rest before we land. Before you sit down – I noticed you were speaking to the singing man in 12C. May I ask what he said?"

The father was quiet for a moment. He leaned toward Nicole so he could speak quietly over the engines. "He said he thought Todd was sick. He said he felt warm. He also said the baby seemed small, which I thought was a weird thing to say about a baby, but he said he meant that the baby felt skinny. He's nine months. He thought we should try to find the first aid place in the terminal to at least get his temperature taken. He said he wasn't a doctor but there was something about the sound of the cry that was off. He even said he thought we should see a pediatrician right away."

"There is a small clinic, kind of a first-aid station, at the upper level in the Bradley Terminal, that's Terminal B," Nicole said. "There are signs and if you can wait just a moment, after we land I can help you find it."

"Thanks," the father said. "His mother isn't going to want to do that."

Nicole smoothed the baby's hair with affection, but it gave her a chance to feel its forehead. "I'm not a baby expert either," she said. "But he does feel warmer than I would expect a baby to feel." And she could see that the baby did not look like a plump nine-month-old.

Out of the corner of her eye she detected the mother's glare.

"What do you think we should do?" the man said.

"I wouldn't want to tell you how to care for your sweet beautiful boy," she said. "But I would do what the man in

12C said. Get his temp taken here at the airport and get him to your pediatrician right away."

"We don't actually have one at this time," the man said, tilting his head slightly toward his glowering wife.

Her years of dealing with unreasonable passengers had reduced Nicole's tolerance for fools inflight or earthbound to single-digit levels on any scale she imagined might exist. "Well, as I say, it's your and your wife's business, but" – she put her ear right up to the father's to make her point forcefully but beyond mom's range – "get a temperature read on this sweetheart at Terminal B the minute we land, then get yourself to a pediatrician pronto, and I mean a reputable one, not one of those homeopathic guys." She added, glancing down at grumpywife, "And don't take no for an answer."

The father nodded and smiled sadly, said *thanks*, and scootched past 5D to return to his middle seat. Mom reached for baby Todd, but the father said something to her with some firmness, and kept the child.

The PA crackled. Frederick was broadcasting. "Good morning again, ladies and gentlemen. We're expecting a smooth flight all the rest of the way to Los Angeles on Hemisphair 577 this morning, but before we begin our final service, we wanted to take note of what we believe to be an all-time record. Some of you may have noticed that we had five babies all crying at once after we hit that turbulence, which is probably not a record, but what has to be a record is that a very generous and kind passenger volunteered to quiet each one of those babies and in each case he was successful, as you have all no doubt gratefully noticed.

"Now I do want to go on record that Hemisphair's corporate policy strongly approves of babies and even crying babies. But believe me, the cabin crew is very appreciative of any assistance we get from passengers to make everyone's flight a pleasant one."

12C was chuckling and shaking his head. The mother in the seat next to him, whose baby was still snoozing, was smiling and speaking to him and he was responding pleasantly.

"We don't want to wake up these kiddos," Frederick continued, "but we would like to acknowledge the gentleman in 12C who helped us out with his collection of lullabies. So please – don't applaud. We'd like to ask everyone to please go *ssshhhhhhhh* to say thank you to the amazing gentleman in 12C."

The cabin went *ssshhhhhhhh* and the man in 12C raised his left hand and gave a little wave, and everyone laughed a little.

And Nicole laughed a little but stopped when she saw Carolyn bend over to speak to the man in 12C.

Oh, that is inappropriate. That is inappropriate, Carolyn. You appear to have neglected to button that second button on your top and it is falling dangerously open, but more to the point, only I am allowed to bother the pleasant man in 12C because I discovered him and I may be in the process of developing a crush on him, so I cordially invite you to stand your flirty ass upright and get your tail back to your tail galley.

The man shook his head. *Carolyn, the man said he didn't want anything to drink. Now let's move on and get that serv – WHAT is she doing? What – she's writing something on a card and giving it to him! No class. No class. Giving him your number right in front of the whole cabin. I hope Frederick saw that.*

Carolyn stood and moved to the back of the plane.

Nicole observed that 12C did not turn around and so did not observe Carolyn tossing her nice roundy buns in those tightish navy slacks north and south as the jet continued east to west.

4

HEMISPHAIR 577 WAS on the ground at LAX a few minutes early but sat on the runway waiting for a gate to open up. The man in 12C was dozing. Several of his five little friends had awakened, but seemed refreshed and none offered anything other than normal appealing baby noises.

Nicole thought about the man in 12C. Quiet. Large. Sandy, a pleasant, quiet color for a man who seemed to exist to spread calm and goodwill. Those even, pleasant features she had been studying. Not dramatically handsome. But dramatic handsomeness would have fought with his calming nature, would have distracted the observer from the power of his kindness and quietude; in him, pleasantness had a physical appeal of its own. Still, not a man she would have instantly thought of as her type – just to look at him.

But then, in her life she'd acquired a couple of her type – to look at them. More than a couple if you counted boyfriends. And where were they now?

And the fact was, she hadn't just looked at him.

She had experienced who he was.

The man from 12C had comforted and captivated almost two hundred people by caring for five little ones and didn't require one bit of thanks.

Perhaps, she thought, she was wrong about her type. Or needed to consider the merits of other types.

And . . . something else. When she stood by him as he held the little ones and seemed to enter their world as he breathed his melodies into them, she felt *yes, this is a man I could stand with. A man who makes me feel good to be near.*

No perhaps about it, she decided. The formerly soft and pleasant, now tall and pleasant but also intriguing man in 12C had moved to *romantic suspect* on Nicole's man-meter.

She thought about Aliyah's warning about meeting strange men on planes – some strange because unknown, some strange because just flat strange. Only one way to factor out strangeness, and she settled on her strategy to accomplish it.

Nicole was taking no chances with the crafty Carolyn. She moved up a couple of aisles from the departure door and waited for the man from 12C. The mother from 5F gave her a look as she passed by, but Nicole just smiled and urged her to have a great day. "You too, sir," she said to Todd's father as he passed with the baby and they exchanged a serious glance, "and you too, little fella."

When the man from 12C moved even with Nicole, she touched his arm and he paused almost as though he were expecting it. Nicole retreated into the row so the man could get most of his largeness out of the aisle to let the passengers file out. Some spoke words of thanks or patted his back as they passed by. He acknowledged them, a little nervously, Nicole thought, while he waited for what she had to say. He carried only a small duffle that he lifted out of the aisle.

"A final request," Nicole said. She thought she'd better get to it. "May I ask you to wait for just a few minutes out in the boarding area? I have a few duties here and I'd like to speak with you. I can't let this amazing event go without some kind of wrap-up. I'll be out soon. You don't have to make a short connection, do you?"

The pleasant man seemed pleasantly startled. "No," he said. "LA is it for me today. Uh, sure, I can – I can make a couple calls. I didn't check anything. I don't have to be anywhere – maybe later I do, I don't know yet. It would be – it would be nice to talk to you without having to shout over – over Messrs. Pratt and Whitney roaring twenty feet away. Uh, yeah – sure."

"Great," she said, but she sensed his uncertainty despite his joke about the engines. "I won't be long, thanks for hanging." The big man ducked out the door and moved with the rest of the crowd up the ramp, continuing to receive expressions of gratitude that he deflected with a smile and a *my pleasure* or *no problem*.

"Good move," Frederick said. "That was a flight to remember."

"Did you see Carolyn give him her number?" Nicole said.

"That was a card for a couple of free drinks at the Hemisphair Club," Frederick said. "That was just the manager's name and our flight number. She was going to call and alert him that the guy might stop by and to let him in without an Executive Passport card."

Nicole wished she'd thought of that, but the guy didn't seem like the Hemisphair Club type. She regretted her suspicion of Carolyn for about four seconds. Frederick told her the rest of the crew would finish up and she could go.

The large pleasant man from 12C was sitting in one of the vinyl row-chairs and talking on his phone. He saw her approaching and ended his call.

She sat, leaving a chair between them. Her folded hands may have pulled her hem from her knees, just a little. She hadn't figured out what to say so she turned to face him and started talking to see what would come out.

"I'm usually not this forward," she said, which was usually true, "but I was completely enchanted by what you did back there, and honestly" – she paused and, she was startled to realize, might have batted her eyelashes – "pretty enchanted by you. I'm not allowed to socialize in my uniform but I can change in the crew lounge, get myself together a little. I'd really like to know more about you and I'd like to buy you a cocktail and maybe a snack or something at the bar at Armand's Grill at the Four Seasons? I checked, it's open. Coffee if it's too early for a drink. Do you know it, on Century? Just a few blocks, a cabbie would be happy to have the ride to the hotel. It's nice and quiet, especially this time of day. May I meet you in there in about an hour, give or take? I have a million questions."

The man blinked and did not respond right away, but she thought maybe she saw his pleasant mouth move in the direction of a true smile.

He's not used to getting hit on. I've made this nice guy uncomfortable. Good work, Nikki.

"Sure," he said, after another moment. "Armand's – I've been there. Pretty sure. Yes – I have. I'm going to be short several hundred thousand answers, though."

Nicole was thrilled at this answer, a near-flirtatious response to her unabashed hit.

"Actually," he said. "That would be nice. We did make a good team, didn't we?"

"I don't think I –"

"Oh no no," he said, his face suddenly serious. "I was very glad you were at my – you were there. I was glad you asked me to help."

He looked like he wanted to say more, but was unsure of his words and of the moment.

Nicole broke the pause, saying, "I was happy to be your booking agent."

"I – I hope I can say this – maybe it's too personal, I don't know you," the man said. "But – I noticed something about you. There was – you had – there was a certain – I don't know – joy, I guess – yeah, joy – about the way you went about your business. That little soft-shoe you did with the safety speech, and the way you kind of – I don't know, flourished? – is that the word? brandished? – the little fake seat belt and safety card. You looked like you were glad to be there. I'm sorry, I'm talking too much. Watching you made just me happy. I'm sorry, too much."

"No," Nicole said, "please."

"I know taking care of people is your job. But I just sensed something – extra with you. A – warmth and – and affection for the babies. Also the passengers."

His halting assessment was the way Nicole did feel about the people who flew. "That's sweet," she said. "I try."

"Not 'try,'" he said. "The helping – touching others is natural with you. That was – it was just my sense of you, anyway. Not that you're there to be analyzed. By me. By anyone. I'm talking too much. Too much talking, sorry. I apologize. I'm honored and flattered by your invitation. I'm not much of a talker. Or –" he chuckled – "I wasn't until now."

When they stood, she got on her toes and kissed him

lightly on the cheek; but not a kiss, really, just a close brush making the kissnoise, not even enough to leave a trace of the lipstick she'd reapplied when the plane touched down, but she hoped no supervisor noticed anyway. She turned and moved quickly away without checking his reaction, her rolling crew kit trailing behind her clicking heels.

She knew he wouldn't stand her up, talker or not. He would be there.

Yes, a million questions:

What were you singing?
Are you a singer?
What do you do for a living?
Do you live in Los Angeles?
Fly much?
What's going on in Dallas?
Do you take this flight often?
What was that big book?
Where do you have to be later?
Married?
Girlfriend?
How do you know about babies?
I have trouble sleeping sometimes. At night.
I don't cry much, but sometimes.
Will you sing me a song sometime?
What's your name?

In the crew lounge, Nicole changed and washed her face and reapplied her makeup, but only a light treatment, clean and natural around the eyes, and super easy on the blush. Lips, not so red as before. She unpinned her hair and shook it down around her face and shoulders and brushed the morning's remaining L'Oreal out of it. She replaced the solitaire sparkler around her neck with a feathery Navajo design she'd bought in Taos and been waiting for the right moment to wear.

She considered this unfamiliar look in the mirror and decided she liked it.

Her thoughts turned to the minidate she'd just improvised with the man from 12C.

The whole thing gave her a soft, pleasant feeling.

5

SHE SCANNED THE giant horseshoe bar at Armand's. A few early afternoon drinkers, but even in the dimness of the room she could see that the big pleasant man was not among them.

"May I help you, ma'am?" The hostess cuddled a sheaf of enormous laminated menus in both arms. "We will be serving lunch until 2, but the bar will be open."

Nicole craned her neck to look into the main dining room. Some late lunchers wrapping up; but no.

"I'm supposed to meet someone here," she said. "He's tall. Maybe with a small duffel."

She felt her day sinking. Her blunt approach, the almost-kiss, had been wrong. He spoke sweetly to her and he had seen something in her that she felt in herself, but it was hard for him, he wasn't used to it. He almost couldn't get it out.

She had no name. She had nothing. She could have gotten his name from Frederick; he had all the passengers' names by seat. Stupid to have forgotten that. As she stood there feeling foolish with her soft pretty new look she was left with the mystery of the pleasant man, not himself soft as she had first thought, but soft of soul, a man who seemed to understand the hidden miseries of the helpless and the wordless.

And he was a little wordless himself.

Nice going, Nikki.

"No one has checked in," the hostess said. "You're welcome to look around."

There was smoke and honey in the voice over Nicole's right shoulder:

The blue sky is blue
But it's not gloomy

Nicole spun to face the big pleasant man, who had come up behind her.

If lifts you up
It brings you to me

"Oh," she said. "I—."

He looked down at her. His pleasant expression had deepened, turned playful but serious, warm and happy and – what? – searching her eyes for what comfort and ease she might need and he might offer. Looking for a place to settle; perhaps searching for calm and rest himself.

He took a breath and bent to her ear.

We fly
And the clouds will part for us

We soar
And dream a single heart for us

The lyrics rolled out slowly, the melody gently approaching and receding like the Malibu sea-margin at change of tide.

The world may cry
With unknown sorrow
Just close your eyes
Until tomorrow

He stopped. His lips brushed her ear, her hair, as he rose from her.

She had not expected the warmth of this greeting, or the drama of his surprise. Perhaps her forwardness had reached him after all, shook something loose in that big body.

He knows me. He feels me. He feels us. It is a beginning.
Be cool.

"It's beautiful," she said.

His mouth opened, but he was silent. His eyes remained on hers, unblinking, but they sparkled in the reflection from the bar lamps.

Nicole said, "Is that what you were singing to the babies?"

He shook his head.

"I don't know it," she said, "but the melody and the words, it's just gorgeous and moving. Your voice — it's so deep and filled with air, like a tree would sing in a breeze. And the song is so perfect for our morning with the babes."

The big pleasant man nodded, and grew soft again.

Nicole's eyes began to fill.

A beginning.

She knew, but she asked: "Who wrote that?"

"I did," he said. "Just now."

[END]

Made in the USA
Columbia, SC
06 August 2021